Noah Brooks

Tales of the Maine Coast

Noah Brooks

Tales of the Maine Coast

ISBN/EAN: 9783337068387

Printed in Europe, USA, Canada, Australia, Japan

Cover: Foto ©Andreas Hilbeck / pixelio.de

More available books at **www.hansebooks.com**

Tales of
The Maine Coast

NOAH BROOKS

CHARLES SCRIBNER'S SONS
1894

CONTENTS

THE setting of these short tales is mainly in and around the ancient town of Castine, Me., thinly disguised under the name of " Fairport." That town was the birthplace and is the present habitation of the author, who has sketched many of his characters from real life. All of the stories were written as diversions at infrequent intervals during the later years of a busy life with the hope that readers may find in them the same recreation that the writer has, and at the same time gain some notion of the characteristics of the people and the natural scenery of the Maine coast.

Pansy Pegg

ل

PANSY PEGG

HER real name was Nance. There is no tradition extant that she was ever called Nancy. Her mother, who drifted to Fairport more that fifty years ago, brought with her as baggage a bulging bandbox stuffed with clothing, two chairs, a bedstead, and Nance, then an infant in arms. The full name of Mrs. Pegg was never known to the Fairport public. When she ran aground, so to speak, on the shore of Oakum Bay, Fairport, she wore a gown of homespun cotton - and - woollen stuff locally named linsey-woolsey, skimped in the skirt and dyed with sumach. This much-enduring garment was Mrs. Pegg's only robe, from the day of her landing to the day of her death, which happened some ten years later ; and as Linsey Woolsey Pegg, or more commonly Linsey Woolsey, she was subsequently celebrated in the annals of the town.

When Linsey Woolsey gave a name to her fatherless offspring, that turbulent infant was dipped in the briny waters of Oakum Bay and was then and there christened Nance. "Just Nance," said her mother, wearily, when asked if that was all she had to give the child. "Just Nance, and nothin' more." And by that curt name she was thereafter called.

That part of the saline shore of Fairport which lies between Jarvis's and Perkins's wharves, sweeping inward with a flattened curve a scant eighth of a mile, was and is known as Oakum Bay. There were the sailor boarding-houses, there the coasting and fishing schooners of the port were beached for submarine repairs, and there was the wide-doored boat-house where three or four old women sat in the sun spinning into yarn the oakum picked from ropes and cables that had been weathered by gales off Cape Horn, bleached in the fiery suns of India and the South Pacific or mildewed by the everlasting fogs of the Grand Banks. Were they endowed with power of speech, full many a tale of perilous adventure might these fragments of rigging tell as they ignobly passed into their last estate of plebeian oakum to calk withal the seams of the humble craft of the port.

Water Street here skirts the inner edge of the little bay, dustily or muddily meandering along

the bluffy bank that overhangs the beach. At
odd intervals on the crumbling marge of this
ragged bank were dotted the weather-beaten
shelters of the oakum-pickers and fisher folk.
There was a long-timbered box-like structure in
which were steamed to flexibility the planks
used in patching vessels' hulls, and here and
there a time-stained cot or shabby hovel clung
desperately to the steep edge, supported on its
seaward side by tall stilts, which, like strad-
dling legs, grotesquely sprawled along the shore.
The beach was garnished with sea - drift of
every imaginable description. Here was a tar-
kettle, there a lobster-pot, an aged pound-net,
the skeleton of an ancient jolly-boat, the battered figure-head of a once-proud ship, now the
sport of village children, and here a sheave-
block or a tangle of running rigging. These bits
of wrack and waste, mingled with sun-whitened
seaweed and eel-grass, imparted to the classic
shores that indescribable marine flavor which is
an everlasting memory to each wandering son
and daughter of the coast of Maine. The faint
odor of tar, the subtle aroma of dripping kelp,
the mingled bouquet of various submarine
growths and shore-born things have followed
these far-wandering nomads to the uttermost
parts of the earth. There, too, one hundred

5

feet or so from low-water mark, lay the bones of the British transport St. Helena, sunk in the War of the Revolution, and now dived for by the amphibious residents of the bay, who turn an honest penny by selling to summer visitors great chunks of solid English oak, black and iridescent in the sea-change that has passed through them in their century-long submersion in the brine.

When Nance Pegg was ten years old her mother, the faded Linsey Woolsey, gave up a futile struggle for existence, and bequeathing to the town her unpaid rent-bill, her poverty-stricken outfit, and Nance, was carried up Windmill Hill to sleep as comfortably as she might in the sandy soil of the village graveyard. Nance, now become a charge upon the tax-payers, would have been sent to the town poor-house, across the harbor, but the shrewd eyes of Marm Skinner, who kept the sailor boarding-house, at the head of Jarvis's wharf, were upon the child, and at that thrifty lady's request, Nance was bound out to her by the selectmen ; and so the girl entered on a life of drudgery as the slave of Marm Skinner, at the beck and call of a motley crew of sailor-men in the boarding-house. Nance grew sturdily into a maidenhood which was more boyish than girlish. Nobody could guess what mixture of alien blood had made in this offspring of the American Linsey Woolsey so strange a child of the sun. From her earliest and most rebellious infancy she had refused to wear any headgear whatever. In heat or cold, sunshine or shower, winter or summer, Nance went bareheaded. Her skin, roughened and reddened by exposure, might have been very beautiful; her profile, regular and aquiline, could not be marred by any neglect of her own. Her crowning glory might have been her hair, which was silky and abundant and had that auburn-red hue which is sometimes called Titianesque. But Nance's perversity wellnigh destroyed its beauty. It is said that the Russian peasant covers his head with a wooden bowl, and the barber's shears cut short off all that part of the crop that hangs below the edge of the covering. Nance's hair, which was parted on one side, man-fashion, was dressed in the Russian manner.

Little cared Nance Pegg for the rude jocularity of the boys, the disdainful looks of the girls, or the pitying glances of the elder Fairport folk at her quaint and unlovely appearance. Nimble-witted, sharp-tongued, and ready, under provocation, for a tilt in wordy warfare with anybody, Nance grew up to be at once the

terror and the amusement of Oakum Bay. Indeed, her fame, like her lithe and flitting
presence, transcended the bounds of the little
settlement on the shore and pervaded the entire
township by the sea. Not even Squire Atherton, the solemn and austere first selectman of
Fairport, or Parson Mason, the spiritual head
of the community, nor Philip Rowell, town
clerk, was so well-known a public character
as Nance Pegg, the orphaned child of the sea
and the sun.

The girl was an adept in all the arts and avo-
cations of the shore folk. She disdained to row
in any other fashion than cross - handed ; she
knew the times and seasons, the habits and
the goings and comings of all manner of wild
fowl and fish, from the ululating and melan-
choly loon or the high - flying wild goose to
the capricious mackerel and meditative clam.
Versed in sea lore, she knew the name of each
mast and sail and rope of the craft that navi-
gated the waters of the bay, and could accurate-
ly describe the rig and build of every kind of
vessel that sails the sea. A strong and wiry
frame gave her power of endurance, and no
fatigue appeared to fret her, no heat or cold
dismay her ; and he must be a tough and vent-
uresome lad who dared to challenge the lightly

8

clad Nance to a swimming match in the chill
waters of the bay at any time of the year.   Sent
by Marm Skinner on errands to the village
stores, she usually trundled before her a wheelbarrow which when empty twirled and whirled
before as she went, in very wantonness of phys-
ical strength.   Decent matrons and maids
were often scandalized by hearing Nance, as
she passed about the town on divers errands
bent, drumming with agile fingers on tin pan or
pail and keeping time thereto with her own
shrill and melodious whistle.

The girl was stubborn but never wayward, and
she grew up big and masculine, more and more
wilful, and in her developed a certain dominant
beauty which began to attract the notice of the
young sailors and fishermen of the port.   Even
these rude critics said that her only charm was
in her eyes, which were changeful in their moods,
now blazing like sapphires in their wrath and
now tenderly violet in rare access of sentiment
or yearning.   But for the most part she was a
rigid stoic.   She hated every evidence of feminine weakness or gentleness, scorned the pretty
arts of needlework, and commented with acer-
bity on the dress and manners of the village
maids, thereby delighting the sailor folk who ate
at Marm Skinner's table.   "'Their riggin' costs

more than the hull," was Nance's caustic remark, as she placed on the board a smoking dish
of beef-and-greens. "And they scud back to
harbor at the fust sign of a squall," she continued sententiously. A party of gay pleasure-
seekers were passing by the windows of the
house, and a bearded sailor-man had asked her
why she did not array herself like one of these.
"No good," she sniffed, with her aquiline nose
in the air. "No good for keeps."

But a change was awaiting this waif of the
shore. Aunt Doty Perkins, the busy, bustling
manager of the village tavern that stood among
the elms at the foot of the Common, thought
to reclaim Nance from her hoydenish ways.
Madam Perkins was a generous person, ample of
bulk, kind of heart, and surreptitiously given to
certain sentimental vagaries that did not fit in
with her housewifely qualities and hard common-
sense. Her motherly heart had been touched
by the forlornness of the lot of the poor waif of
Oakum Bay, and she longed to take the girl, so
unfriended and neglected, into a softer atmosphere and more homelike surroundings where,
as she phrased it, the girl might be made something of. There had been a small rebellion in
Marm Skinner's boarding-house from which
Nance, now a well-grown girl with an athletic

figure, had emerged victorious, leaving the dame on the field lamenting a broken teapot and an eye bruised and blackened. Nance fled to Madam Perkins, whom she had long since intuitively recognized as her friend. This crisis in the girl's affairs was Madam Perkins's opportunity. Tearfully and wrathfully, Marm Skinner transferred to Madam Perkins Nance's articles of bondage. She told the selectmen that she could do nothing with the " sarcy jade " and these magnates having consented to the deed, the slave of the sailor boarding-house became an inmate of the Hancock Tavern. In these matters Nance took no part and apparently no interest. But when, the legal formalities having been complied with, the transfer was made in due form, Nance entered on her new duties with real enjoyment and gratitude, although outwardly she went about her work with the same stolidity and stoical self-control that had characterized her servitude in the house of entertainment at the head of Jarvis's wharf.

Nance was a tough subject for the humanizing process which Madam Perkins was craftily preparing for her. She clung to her wheelbarrow, her melodious whistle, and to most of her masculine manners ; and, although she consented to wear shoes and stockings and endured with

patience the addition of three inches to the
length of her skirts, she absolutely refused to
have her hair dressed in any other way than the
fashion of the Russian bowl before referred to.
In one respect, however, she underwent a trans-
formation unexpectedly sudden and radical.

" Her name has always been against her,"
said Madam Perkins. " It stands to reason that
a girl born and baptized as Nance was has never
had a living show to be anything but a tomboy,
as she is. Nance! " she uttered with supreme
contempt. " Nance! What decent, self-respecting girl could remain decent and self-respecting
with a name like that? "

So, after much deliberation, and some consultation with a literary friend, Miss Callista
Hatch, Madam Perkins resolved to rechristen
Nance as Pansy. In those days Effie, Mattie,
Tiny, and other baby names, so greatly affected
by a later generation, were not known. They
who were averse to the use of such old-fashioned
girl names as Margaret, Mary, and Jane, usually
inclined to Sophronia, Euphelia, or Constantia,
names dear to the novel-readers of that time.
When it was announced that Nance was to be
known as Pansy Pegg, great was the entertainment of the community. There was something
so grotesque in the association of ideas, the

beautiful flower and the tough girl, something so comic in its alliteration, that the rechristening took the town by storm. The gossips repeated " Pansy Pegg " in unaffected wonderment; the boys yelled the name whenever its wearer made her frequent appearance on the street, and everybody was so tickled with what seemed to be an original joke that the new name was fastened on the girl with marvellous readiness. Before a half year had passed none apparently remembered that Linsey Woolsey's child had ever been other then Pansy Pegg. " Nance " was lost in the waters of oblivion.

The second stage of Pansy's reclamation from tomboyhood was her matriculation in the town school. Heretofore her education had been chiefly confined to a knowledge of the letters of the alphabet taught her by her mother. And under the tutelage of an ancient mariner, laid up for repairs in Marm Skinner's boarding-house after a fall from the yard-arm, she had furtively learned to count as high as one hundred and to combine letters into words of two syllables. In rural New England so light an educational outfit as this would be regarded as wickedly meagre, even for the humblest of longshore folk; it was shamefully deficient for a Pansy. Education is generally accepted as the substitute for all shortcomings, and it was resolved that Pansy Pegg's rehabilitation required at least a fair proficiency in reading, writing, and arithmetic.

When Madam Perkins announced her intention to send Pansy to school it was popularly felt that this was another evidence of the bounteous generosity of the landlady of the Hancock Tavern. Such odd jobs of housework as the girl could despatch "between schools," or early in the morning, or later in the day, were to be all her tasks. When the chores were done up and the nine-o'clock school-bell rang, Pansy would fare forth to the springs of knowledge that gushed forth on the Common under the patronage of the Town School Committee. It was Madam Perkins's wish that Pansy should be a pupil of Miss Maria Jane Bates, the elderly spinster, well-seasoned in school-teaching, then administering the terrors of the primary department of the town-school system in the antique structure in Dresser's Lane. In those remote days, graded schools were unknown in Fairport; there was but a step between the mistress's school taught by Miss Maria Jane and the master's school presided over (as the modern phrase goes) by Mr. Adoniram Judson Woods. Scholars advanced to the Rule of Three in arithmetic and to the American First Class Book in reading, or no longer amenable to the discipline of a woman teacher, were promoted to the master's school at once. Across this line Pansy could not go by merit of her arithmetic or her reading.

"Law sakes alive, Mis' Perkins!" said Miss Callista, called in council on the question of poor Pansy's disposal in school. "Law sakes alive! Pansy 'll never stand it for a day with Maria Jane Bates. She'll be sure to raise a rumpus before she has been inside the Dresser's Lane school an hour, she's so big and unruly; and she hates the women folks so. She'll be sure to say or do somethin' to rile up Maria Jane; and you know how quick-tempered Maria Jane is. There'll be a tussle sure; who'll get the worst of it there's no tellin'; but it won't be Pansy, I guess."

Miss Callista grimly smiled as she thought of Pansy Pegg wrestling with the small and lame schoolmistress, whose sharp temper and yet sharper tongue held in check an unruly flock of children who feared the slight little woman more than they would have feared the awful master of the school on the Common.

"Well, I'm sure I don't know," sighed the good landlady of the Hancock Tavern. "Pansy is a master hand to work, and they do say that she's just as good a fighter as she is a worker;

and if she should ever tackle Maria Jane Bates, the Lord have mercy on Maria Jane. But I do rely on Maria Jane's moral 'suasion. She's a lady born and bred. Her mother was a Black, of the down-Bluehill-way Blacks, you know, and her father was own cousin to Squire Atherton. I've counted a good deal on Maria Jane's example and softenin' influence on Pansy."

"Softenin' influence," repeated Miss Callista, sardonically. "Maria Jane Bates is as sour as a vinegar cruet, and she does nothin' from the time school's took in until the time it's let out but scold, scold, scold ; and they do say that when she gets home she keeps up her everlasting clack until her poor old bedridden father layin' there in the ell-part of the house calls to them to shet the door until the squall blows out. Softenin' influence ! Oh, land ! "

Madam Perkins, though with many misgivings in her mind, still argued that with the schoolmistress was a more hopeful outlook for the rampagious and obstreperous Pansy. The harsh discipline of the master's school she dreaded. She was not willing to give up the prospective refinement which she had expected for her difficult charge. But with many a sigh and many a prayer that all would turn out for the best, she sent the girl to the school on the Common.

The appearance of Pansy Pegg in that institution of learning was a keenly enjoyed sensation for the scholars. The big girls on the high back seats on their side of the school-house, which faced the entrance, gazed with elegant and superior scorn on the new-comer. The little girls farther down in dignity and on the plane that sloped to the centre of the school floor, giggled behind their books and put out their tongues at Pansy when the master's attention was directed at the stranger. The boys on the other side of the room at once recognizing an enemy, coughed derisively, and for a moment appeared to have entered the early stages of pulmonary consumption. Mr. Adoniram Judson Woods, a very small man, with very small white hands and mild blue eyes, perched on his high stool behind his desk, sharply rapped for order and cried " Silence ! " then colored red to the roots of his thin and flax-colored hair. The schoolmaster, despite his reputation for severity, was as sensitive as any one of his girl pupils.

Only Pansy Pegg, who had stirred this wave of feeling, remained unmoved. Guided by a motion of the master's ferule, or ruler, as it was more generally called, she strode across the floor space between the girls' side and the boys' side of the school-room and crowded herself, with a feeble attempt at a grin, into the cramped seat and desk assigned to her. Pansy was bigger than the biggest girl in the school. To the smaller scholars she appeared gigantic. And the incongruousness of this great girl squeezed into a narrow seat intended for the youngest of scholars just emancipated from the thraldom of the schoolmistress, was comic, as comic as Pansy Pegg could well be. Some of the bigger boys humorously shuffled their feet on the sanded floor by way of showing that they appreciated the fun of the situation; and Mosey Ellis, a peachy-cheeked mite of a boy, ironically known as "Goliah," snorted with infantile glee; whereupon he was austerely directed by the master to stay after school at noon, a dictum which Mosey tearfully accepted as equivalent to an order for ten blows with the ruler on the ampler part of his small person, or five blows with the rattan on his bare hand, as the dread tyrant might capriciously decide thereafter.

Poor Pansy was not only the biggest girl, but she was the lowest scholar in the school. She sat in the lowest seat of all, and she was so low down in the classification of the pupils that she was a class by herself. Even the youngest of the little tots around her regarded her with ill-concealed wonder as she laboriously floundered through "bias," "borax," "butler," "bridal," "climax," and so on, in the two-syllabled words in the fifth chapter of the National Spelling Book, in which her first lessons were cast. But Pansy, if she noted any of these things, showed no sign of what she thought of them. The grim old cast-iron stove in the middle of the school-room was not more impassive than her countenance. She conscientiously labored to read and spell when, in her "freshman class of one," she stood up at the master's call and went through her lessons. She was constant at school, and although she looked full oft with a quaking heart through the aperture cut in one of the panels of the tavern kitchen-door to give a view of the face of the clock in the dining-room, to note the fateful movements of the hands toward school-time, she never required from the landlady one of those written "excuses" to which other scholars resorted in frequent weakness of spirit. In her dumb and undemonstrative way she appreciated Madam Perkins's kindly meant intentions to humanize her.

But the spirit of mischief was strong upon her, and no sooner had Pansy become wonted to the strange environment of the school-house

than this began to assert itself. In her inmost
heart she despised the school, the master, the
books and lessons, the boys—and especially the
girls, with a contempt too deep for measure-
ment. She was skilled in all manner of small
and vexing games; and although nobody ever
brought home to her door any serious mischief
wrought, it was never for an instant doubted
that the knotting of the school bell-rope, the
overturning of the bell, the tarring of the master's ruler, the torturing pins in the boys' seats,
the water in their ink-stands, and the multifari-
ous and endless trickeries of the schoolhouse
were all of Pansy. She was one of those rare
girls who can throw a stone like a boy, and
certain was her aim at any target whatever.
Thereby she fell.

Spit-balls, made of paper chewed fine and
hard, were lawful ammunition among the boys,
but were abhorred by the girls and were inex-
orably banned by the authorities. To Mr.
Adoniram Judson Woods a spit-ball was in-
cendiary, insubordinate, devilish. A boy detected in the act of making or firing a spit-ball
was simply whaled; a mere whipping was not
sufficiently condign for his offence. If Master
Woods could have revived the rope's-end
soaked in brine which had been one of the

instruments of torture under a previous administration, but now prohibited, he would have
reserved that punishment for the spit - ball
player. Pansy Pegg excelled in the art of
making and firing spit-balls. She had a deft
way of flipping with thumb and finger one of
these projectiles, masticated to the hardness of
a bullet, with such accuracy of aim that the
mark was never missed. Watching her opportunity when the master's attention was
diverted for an instant, she would stealthily
raise her right hand with thumb and fore-
finger charged, snap the ball, which sped like a
white flash to some poor wretch's ear or eye,
he the while delving in book or atlas, unconscious of harm. There would be a half-sup-
pressed yell of pain, or a surprised cry of
" Ouch ! " and everybody knew that the victim
had been shot with a spit-ball by Pansy Pegg.
But Pansy, with her eyes demurely dropped
upon her book, as she sat facing the wooden
wainscot of her corner, was apparently as unconscious of the fierce inquisition for the as-
sailant as if she were solitarily wading the cool
waters of Oakum Bay or from her eyrie at the
head of Jarvis's wharf was watching the spin-
ners in the sun.

Or a flight of more juicy and thoroughly

masticated spit-balls would bombard the ceiling over the master's desk until it resembled a stuccoed space irregularly embossed with flat rosettes of plaster. Pansy scorned to spit-ball the girls. Poor things, she thought, they could not fire back; and they would tell. That was the boys' one virtue: they would not tell.

But long impunity had made Pansy over-bold. One fatal day she was caught by the master in the very act of projecting a wad of chewed paper which hit Joe Murch in the hollow of the ear and made him roar. It was a wonderful shot, for Joe's seat was full twenty feet away from Pansy's, and the bullet had hit the mark with inerrant speed. But this surprising expertness did not save the marksman from the punishment which the master had long before hung over her head. Girls were not " rulered " in that school. Pansy, however, being an exceptional transgressor, had been warned that if she were ever detected in the act of firing spit-balls, she would be punished corporeally; she must now meet her fate. She sullenly wondered whether it would be the ruler or the rattan, as the schoolmaster lectured her, there standing big and red, with downcast eyes, before the whole school.

Adoniram Judson Woods, with a fluttering heart quivering in his little body, went to the desk and took out his rattan. He felt that the eyes of his flock, especially the eyes of the big girls in the back seats, were upon him, and his dignity must be preserved at any cost.

"Hold out your hand," he commanded with shrill sternness, for his voice, like his person, was small. Pansy extended her hand, red with much dish-washing and roughened by mannish toil. For a moment, in her ready obedience, she seemed to tower far above the little white schoolmaster, she, the biggest and bravest girl in the school. There was a swish and the sharp rattan cut sharply across Pansy's palm.

One or two of the little girls said "Oh!" with involuntary sympathy, and Sophronia Crawford, a large girl, for whose favor the master was popularly believed to hanker, burst into audible weeping. Never once flinching, Pansy, flushed with anger and pain, rubbed her hand on her gown and waited. "Hold it out again," the schoolmaster ordered in his deepest tenor voice. Pansy received the second blow, then swiftly clutching in the air, she seized the tingling rattan, snatched it from the master's surprised grasp and with it dealt him two resounding thwacks on his thinly thatched head.

With bated breath, every boy and girl, big
and little, looked on as Pansy, having given
the master "as good as he sent," handed him
back his rattan, awkwardly courtesying as she
did so.   Master Woods, pale and red by turns
no more, but inflamed to a brilliant crimson
that glowed through his flaxen hair like the
northern lights on the snow, flew at Pansy in
a very ecstasy of wrath.   He rained blows over
her head, her arms, her hands, and her shoulders·
until nearly every girl in school was loudly crying with terror and even the larger boys quaked
with fear.

Then Dave Booden, a mighty fisher lad, of
nearly twenty years, arose in his place in the
high back seats, and striding noisily down the
aisle, said, "See here, mister, this ere thing
has gone fur enough," and took the rattan from
the master's nerveless hold.

"Sho! You just mind your own business,
you great big lubber," said Pansy Pegg,
angrily.   "Leave him to me, can't you?"
With that Pansy collared the master with both
her hands and in one movement easily threw
him over among the seats and desks behind her.
While the poor man was gathering himself together, Pansy stalked out of the school-room,
snatched a fearful joy in one look of farewell as

24

she swiftly swept with her eye the tumultuous brood of scholars, and so disappeared forever out of the purview of Mr. Woods.

On that day Pansy Pegg was eighteen years old. She was absolved from the bondage of the selectmen, her own mistress.

Mrs. Doty Perkins was entertaining a few choice friends in the parlor of the inn with roseate reports of Pansy's present condition of beatitude, her future prospects of attaining complete ladyhood, and her tractable disposition, when the unhappy and enraged subject of her praise stole in at the back door. It was in the middle of the afternoon, and school had just been called in from recess when Pansy's encounter with the master took place. The lull in the household affairs of the tavern gave the girl opportunity to tiptoe her way to the kitchen chamber, where she had made her lair. Sweeping up her scant array of personal belongings, Pansy threw them into a sea-chest which had been bequeathed to her by an old rover of the deep, years before; then she closed and locked it and sat down on its sky-blue lid to think.

"Lucky I'm a free gal now," she muttered. "Them darned selectmen hev no more power over me. That's great! Wish I could feel to

go in and say good-by to Mis' Perkins. But
no ; that'd never do. She'll be down on me
like a thousand o' brick fer pitchin' into the
schoolmaster. Didn't he look scart ! '' And
Pansy rocked herself with glee, sitting there on
the blue sea-chest.

'' I must be stirrin','' she continued, turning
an ear to the door and listening to the murmur
of voices of the gossips in the foreroom below.
'' But where? Land o' Goshen ! Hev I got
to go back to Marm Skinner's ? There ain't
nobody else'll take me in ; and I'm not sartin
shore thet she's forgiven me yet for the peltin' I
gin her when I quit. Oh, my ! oh, my ! what a
mess she wuz in when I left her ! '' And Pansy
chuckled again as she recalled Marm Skinner's discomfiture, the while rubbing her knees
in mirthfulness. The action drew her attention to her right hand, still smarting with pain ;
she regarded its palm crossed with two crimson
welts, and tears of wrath stood in her eyes.

'' The everlastin' peak-nosed, tow-headed,
pernickity little runt ! I'll git even with him
yet ! See 'f I don't ! '' Then recollecting
that she had given the schoolmaster a great deal
more than he sent, considering all things, she
laughed softly to herself and turned her thoughts
once more to her cloudy future.

" Dave Booden, he said Marm Skinner didn't
bear me no grudge," and the girl's cheek
slightly deepened in color as Dave's name
brought before her a vivid picture of the big
fisher lad's sudden appearance on the school-
room field of battle. "Dave knows; but he
had no call to put his oar into my tussle with
the schoolmaster. I hev a great mind to try
old Marm Skinner ag'in as ever I had to eat!"

Pansy knitted her brow in profound thought.
The susurrus of soft voices below, as the
ladies departed by the front door, hastened her
resolution. She rose tumultuously, made a
farewell grimace at her reflection in the little
looking-glass on the wall, and glancing about
the chamber as if to be sure that none heard
her, said, in a loud, emphatic whisper, "I'll do
it, if it takes a leg!"

How Pansy made her peace with Marm
Skinner, none but themselves ever knew. The
elder woman had an eye to her own advantage.
Pansy was indeed a master hand to work. The
machinery of the boarding-house had never run
so smoothly since her departure on the enter-
prise of being made a lady of; and the months
that had intervened had mitigated Mrs. Skinner's
rage and had wiped away the blackness from
under her eye. She bore the girl no malice,

and in view of her undeniable household use-
fulness, was ready to let bygones be bygones.
Sure enough, Dave knew.

It was Dave who went up to the Hancock
Tavern that night with Pansy's old wheelbarrow and brought away the sea-chest contain-
ing her slender kit.   It was Dave who told the
grieving Madam Perkins that Pansy had taken
up her abode again with Marm Skinner ; and
it was to Dave that Madam Perkins first de-
livered her severe remark concerning poor
Pansy's fall from grace—" Like a sow that was
washed returned to her wallowing in the mire "
—a scriptural illustration whose aptness so
tickled the good lady's fancy that she used it
for weeks afterward whenever she had occasion
to refer to the girl's ignominious flight.

When the school had been dismissed that
day, Sophronia Crawford had dropped into the
tavern on her way home, quite by accident, to
borrow from Madam Perkins her famed recipe
for making rice-coral work, and in an entirely
incidental manner had narrated to the astonished landlady the entertaining and exciting
drama played by Pansy Pegg and the schoolmaster, with Dave Booden looming in the final
tableau.   The dame listened with many ohs
and ahs, and when the tale was done and she

had absorbed the last scrap of information from
her artless visitor, she hurriedly gathered up
her ample skirts and mounted to Pansy's
chamber. The clothes-pegs on the wall were
bare; every trace of Pansy's occupation of the
room was gone, save the chest.

"Locked and the key gone, as sure as I'm
a living sinner," murmured the good lady, sinking heavily on the sky-blue chest and sobbing
hysterically. Sophronia, who had doubtfully
followed upstairs, afraid of being intrusive, but
anxious to learn all the details of the flight, for
retail purposes, stood irresolute in the doorway
and wiped a sympathetic tear. "Locked and
the key gone!" repeated Madam Perkins,
more in sorrow than in anger. "I should hate
dreadfully to have anybody suppose I failed of
doing my whole duty by that minx. I'm sure
I done my best for her. I'm sure I did. But
'we may give advice, but we can't give con-
duct,' as Poor Richard says." So saying, the
dame rose with decision and wiped Pansy Pegg
forever from her books.

Pansy's adventure with the schoolmaster was
the topic of conversation at all the tea-tables of
Fairport that evening. Boys so fortunate as to
have seen the scrimmage related its particulars
to less-favored comrades, who listened with envi-

ous greed to the highly ornamented tale. Before the nine o'clock curfew rang, the story of the day had passed into the traditions of the town, never more to be forgotten.

Pansy got even with the schoolmaster later in that very year. In those days when the steamboat, that twice a week brought its passengers from Portland, arrived at the village wharf, the greater part of the population of Fairport went down to see who had come and who was going "to the east'ard" that day. This pleasant custom, which has not altogether fallen into disuse, crowded the old and weather-beaten wharf with gentle bustle and afforded the people an occasion for social interchange rather more agreeable than the distribution of the daily mail at the village post-office.

The T. F. Secor was discharging her passengers and freight one chilly November Saturday afternoon, the clamor of her escaping steam drowning the buzz of conversation and the music of greetings and farewells of comers and goers. The last warning of "All aboard!" had been shouted at the gang-plank, when there was a sudden rush to one side of the wharf and somebody cried "The schoolmaster's overboard!"

Those who, at imminent peril of their own

safety, reached the edge of the dock in time saw the white-headed little schoolmaster helplessly floundering in the water. While some bawled loudly for a boat-hook, others for a line, and others for information as to the master's proficiency in the art of swimming, there was a flash of calico, a gleam of red-flannel petticoat in the air, and Pansy Pegg skilfully struck the water close by the drowning man's side.

"Grab on to my shoulders," said the girl in a low and quiet voice. "Grab on to my shoulders and don't get scart."

The schoolmaster, choking with brine and blowing, as David Booden subsequently remarked, "like a porpuss," meekly obeyed and was borne triumphantly ashore by Pansy, who, as soon as she felt the shallow bottom beneath her feet, shook off the master's embrace, waded to the beach, and having wrung her scant skirts of their dripping burden, stalked grimly homeward along the water-front.

"Three cheers for Nance Pegg!" cried an enthusiastic sailor-man, who having spent most of his time at sea, had never quite accustomed himself to the girl's new name. The cheers were given lustily, as if the cheerers enjoyed this exciting episode very much indeed. Pansy waved her hand with grave jocosity and dis-

appeared around the corner of the wharf build-
ings, her wet skirts clinging to her athletic
limbs.

"The pesky fool," she muttered to herself,
"what did he want to go philanderin' about
that ere string-piece fer? That's what I'd like
to know. I said I'd get even with him. Well,
I hev." And Pansy laughed to herself as she
homeward swished her watery way.

It can hardly be said that Pansy's chivalrous
exploit rehabilitated her in the esteem of the
community; but much of the obloquy which
she had incurred by reason of her unfeminine
assault on the schoolmaster was cancelled by
her gallant rescue of that functionary. As for
Master Woods, himself, he showed his gratitude
by sending to the girl a handsome copy of
"Friendship's Offering," a literary annual highly esteemed by the ladies and gentlemen of that
day. On the fly-leaf of the book were written
the names of the donor and the donee, with an
appropriate quotation in Latin, all of which,
inscribed in a fair, round hand, Pansy regarded
with sardonic mirth, not unmixed with a feeling
of awe. When she had studied the engravings
in this work of art, she put it carefully away in
the bottom of her sea-chest, wrapped in a red-
silk handkerchief, a gift from Dave Booden—

possessions too choice for human nature's daily use.

David, be it said, was so entranced by Pansy's adventure in the salt sea-wave that he exceedingly regretted that he had already christened his new sail-boat the Whisper; if it were not too late he would call her the Pansy. But Dave could not now make a change of name without awaking the derision of his comrades and fellow - craftsmen of Oakum Bay. Fairport was just passing from the sleepiness of an old town that has lost its commerce to the more feverish activity and smartness of a popular summer-resort. Dave was one of the first to take advantage of the new conditions. The Whisper, a sloop-rigged craft, neat in figure, beautiful in model, and lovingly kept in that "ship-shape and Bristol fashion" which delights the eye of the mariner and the marine amateur, was the first pleasure-boat built for hire on Penobscot Bay; and right proud were Dave's friends and neighbors of the graceful craft whose lines, reflected in the tranquil tide of Oakum Bay, roused even the admiration of the undemonstrative Pansy, who intelligently and critically judged her to be "the beautifullest thing afloat."

Whether it was Pansy's fond appreciation of

the Whisper or Dave's undisguised admiration of her prowess that kindled the flame, we may not know; but the community awoke to the fact that "Dave Booden was sweet on Pansy Pegg." Dave was a fine young fellow, good-looking, with ruddy cheeks, curling hair, dark eyes and a manly frame. The young viking, supple, proficient in the rough sports and yet rougher occupations of the shore folk, might well attract the sly admiring glances of the maids of Oakum Bay. Moreover, Dave was known to be forehanded and thrifty. Full of fun and frolic, he was yet a total abstainer at a time and in a community that were not noted for abstemiousness; and although he lent a willing hand when the Green Dragon, an ill-favored resort on Oakum Bay, was mobbed and wrecked, one wild March night, he bore the reputation of a peaceful and law-abiding citizen. And when it was whispered about the port that he was sparking Pansy, the gossips, young and old, lamented that Dave should throw himself away on so tough a customer.

And Pansy? Words cannot fitly express the scorn with which she perceived that Dave was really "making up" to her. It had been forced upon her attention in various ways. When David had sent her, wrapped in pink tissue-paper, a lace collar smuggled from foreign parts by one of the sailors on board the ship St. Leon, she admired the delicate fabric with burning cheeks, spreading it over her red hands; then she put it in her bosom all wrapped as given, and when next she met Dave trundling a barrel of tar along the wharf, she threw his token at him and wildly took to flight. Later in the next spring, one mellow day, while Pansy was setting her room to rights and had opened the window to let in the soft sea-air, a sudden flight of russet apples entering the window in single file called a tell-tale blush to her face; for she knew that nobody but the persistent Dave could have thus paid court to her. Looking out and seeing her suitor gazing expectantly from the steps of the cooper's shop on the beach, she briefly remarked, " Well, I'm gormed ! " and closed her lattice with an injurious clatter.

Pansy was untalkative where her own affairs were concerned, but, like all such self-contained persons, she kept up a busy communion with herself. " The idee," she remarked to her own reflection in the looking-glass — " the idee of Dave Booden's wantin' to keep company 'long o' me ! The idee of *any* feller's wantin' to keep company 'long o' me ! Land sakes alive ! Did you ever ? "

Pansy was grimly interrogating her face in the glass.

"No, and nobody never. Look at them cheeks o' mine, all rough and blowsy-frowsy; pooty good teeth;" and here Pansy grinned widely, the better to regard the pearls in her mouth. "Eyes? Sho! Dave says they are the color of the sea off soundin's; much he knows about a gal's eyes; hair—just look at that air hair! color o' stale mustard, 'n an' all touzled and ez brash ez a bunch o' oakum; and ez fer hands," and Pansy looked ruefully at her overworked but still well-shaped hands, "red ez a b'iled lobster, rough ez a nutmeg-grater. Them pore gal-critters thet traipse round the town with ribbins and furbelows on 'em air what Dave reely wants; only he don't know." Pansy looked down at her faded calico frock, destitute of a furbelow of any sort, and again marvelled at Dave's infatuation.

Nor did personal contact aid David in his suit. Seated by her side on the gunwale of an ancient jolly-boat stranded on the beach of Oakum Bay, one summer night, David, discouraged but still hoping against hope, besought Pansy to reconsider her oft-repeated refusal. It was a rare opportunity. Not often did any young man get near enough to Pansy

Pegg to take her hand in his. But although she had snatched away her fingers from his hold, she did not rudely leave him as had been her wont. The influences of the balmy night, the lapping of the tide upon the pebbly beach, the moonlight glorifying the distant shores of Hainey's Point and Hospital Island and giving an unearthly beauty of color to the gaunt piles of the wharves, bronzed with sea-weed — all these may have touched Pansy's secretive nature where Dave's impassioned words had failed.

The girl sat still, her bold eyes now down-cast and her roving glance noting the small details of the sea-wrack at her feet. She could not take in the possibility that she, the tomboy, the jest of the village, the rude comrade of the rough sailor-men at Marm Skinner's boarding-house, should be the object of any man's love ; and as for this good-looking young fellow at her side, the admiration of all the girls of the bay—pshaw ! the notion was ridiculous, "puffickly rediclus," Pansy had repeatedly said to herself.

" See here, Pansy," hoarsely whispered the love-lorn suitor, " why can't you say yes? It don't make a bit of differ what you think of yourself. I jest think the world and all of you. You're the nicest gal on the bay, bar none !

Bar none!" he repeated with emphasis de-
signed to clinch his assertion. " 'N'f you'd
agree to get spliced, we'd be ez happy ez two
turkle doves, I swan to man we would; 'n' you
know it!" he cried, triumphantly, bending
around and gazing into her averted face. "Ez
happy ez two turkle doves, 'n' you know it.
'N' you know I've got a nice mess of furnitur'
left me by my mother when she died. Why,
when ma slipped her moorin's last fall, Pansy,
and I wuz left alone with them six flag-bottom
chairs and things, d'ye know what I said to
myself?"

Pansy dumbly shook her head.

"Well, I sez to myself 'when Nance sez
yes, them things'—hello! I said 'Nance;'
'scuse me, Pansy, I didn't go for to do it; I
meant to say 'Pansy.' Well, I sez to myself,
sez I, 'them things 'll set us up to housekeepin'
when she sez yes.' Did, honor bright. Now,
if you'll only say yes, jest one little word, y-e-s,
it's a go. Is't a go, Pansy?"

Poor Dave breathed hard. He belonged to
an undemonstrative and little-speaking race.
But he had said a good deal; and so he sighed
and waited.

"No feller can reely think long o' me,"
murmured Pansy, still with averted face. "No

feller reely can. He may think he duz, but he reely duzn't."

" But I do," eagerly replied Dave. "I do, and I reely do. I'm man-grown 'n' I know my own mind. I'm toler'ble well fixed, too ; and the woman that anchors alongside o' me aint agoin' to get neglected or overlooked. Then there's them flag-bottom chairs, six on 'em, and every thing handy about the place even down to the pots and kittles in the cluzzit and the firewood in the shed. Forgive me, Nance, I mean Pansy, fer even namin' the names of them air things, but I do just dote on you, now don't I?"

In answer to this appeal, long and fervid from David Booden, Pansy only bent her head until her thick hair hung like a curtain over her eyes. When she did break silence, she lifted up her face, refined and transfigured in the moonlight, and, looking across the harbor to the misty, spruce-black shores beyond, she said : " I ain't fit to be no man's helpmate. I sh'd hate dretfully to hev the Fairport wimmen-folks pityin' ' pore Dave Booden ' because he'd married a great lubberly tomboy. I sh'd ever-lastin'ly hate to hev them taller-faced gals of the port p'intin' at me 'n' sayin' ' Nance Pegg's in love ! ' Waugh ! the bare thought of it makes

me sick! Nance Pegg in love! Land o'
Goshen! D'ye s'pose I'm a born fool, Dave
Booden? No man-critter shel' ever twit you
with merryin' a pore-house gal; and no gal-
critter shel' ever p'int fingers at me fer bein'
in love; not much, Dave."

Beyond this, Pansy would not go. Not another word could the ardent David allure her
to speak. While he pleaded with simple and
heartfelt eloquence, Pansy rose and, holding
herself as straight as an arrow, went homeward
to Marm Skinner's across the moonlit beach.

And yet, in the solitude of her bed-chamber,
with the door carefully closed, Pansy held up
in her hand a tallow-dip and regarded herself
in the looking-glass. "He called me Nance,"
she said, with a pleased laugh, "'n' he said the
color of my eyes wuz the color of the sea off
soundin's! Much he knows." So saying,
with a sudden flush of redness, she blew out
the light and looked out upon the beach. Dave
was still sitting on the old jolly-boat in an attitude of profound dejection.

"Sorry for Dave," she muttered as she went
to sleep, an hour later.

The mysterious loss of the Whisper is record-
ed in the annals of Fairport. On the day after
Dave Booden's final interview with the obdu-

rate Pansy, he cast off his moorings and slipped
down the harbor, solitary and alone. What
bitter thoughts, what unavailing regrets bore
him company, none can tell. But for these,
Dave was uncompanioned. The sky was blue
and clear over the old port, but a southwest
breeze was stirring and a summer fog was drifting up Penobscot Bay. The eastern end of
Long Island had been blotted from sight when
the Whisper fetched her first long tack over
toward Nautilus Island. Dave's bird-like craft
was standing handsomely out on her westward
reach, well up in the wind's eye, when the fog
shut down at Otter Rock and the white sails
of the Whisper disappeared in the mist, never
more to be seen on the waters of Fairport Harbor and Oakum Bay.

What became of the boat, whether she was
run down in the fog by some bigger craft, or
whether she struck on some one of the sunken
ledges of the bay, or whether Dave sullenly
sailed away and hid himself forever in exile, no
man knows. He was too good a sailor, too
careful a navigator, to be brought to grief while
he had his wits about him. Nevertheless, he
went out of this truthful narrative as completely
as if the sea had opened and engulfed him when
the fog shut down at Otter Rock.

For days and even weeks afterward the
'longshore folk took little thought of Dave's
unexplained absence. It was no unusual thing
for him to spend much time cruising among
the islands of the bay. He had patrons in
Belfast and in Camden who were glad to hire
his boat and his services for a trip up the Penobscot River or to the remoter regions of Somes's
Sound and Bar Harbor. But when the weeks
lengthened into months and the Whisper was
not reported, and the humble cottage by the
beach, where its owner had " kept batch " ever
since his mother died, remained fast locked, it
began to be vaguely hinted about the wharves
that the Whisper, the pride of the port, had
somehow been lost. These murmurs reached
the homes of Fairport, and many whose estate
was far higher than that of the Boodens, sin-
cerely sorrowed over the darkly hinted fate of
the missing man. He was respected, by some
admired ; and the loss of the handsome young
skipper and his favorite boat was in some sense
a public calamity.

"Willin' feller, Dave Booden wuz," said
old Cap'n Eliphalet Grindle, sitting meditative-
ly on the edge of Adams's wharf, nominally
fishing for tomcods, but really "just lazin' the
time away," as his bustling spouse often de-

clared. "Wuz!" he repeated, cautiously looking around to see if any of Dave's intimates
were within earshot. "I might hev said 'is,'
mightn't I, Mister Woods?"

The school-master, whose Saturday afternoons
were chiefly spent, when the weather was pleas-
ent and the tide served, in hopeless and unprofitable angling from the wharf, breathed a sigh
for his ancient and long-forgiven enemy, the
big boy of the town school.

"It is hard to speak of our friends in the
past tense, Captain," he answered, sadly; "but
I greatly fear that the probabilities are all against
the safe return of David. He was a likely
young man. He left no relatives?"

"Nary one, 'cept that jade, Nance Pegg;
'n' she's no relation, unless a gal that's been
courted stiddy goin' on a year or more is likely
to be called kin to the feller that she's sacked.
No, no relations 's fur ez I know on. 'S mother died las' fall. 'S father's lost on the bark Val-
halla; she went onto the Sow-'n-Pigs, Boston
harbor, 'n a gale o' wind—lemme see, 'n 1832,
the cholery year. Haul in yer line, schoolmaster! Ye've got a bite! Sculpin, I guess."

"Smart's a whip, he wuz," continued Cap'n
Grindle, as the master, having disentangled a
wicked-looking sculpin from his hook, baited

and resumed his seat on the string-piece by the
Cap'n. "Smart's a whip, 'n' the only thing
I ever hed ag'in him wuz his gittin' stuck on
that air Nance Pegg. Land o' love ! how any
right-sensed man could git mashed on that big
gawk of a tomboy everlastin'ly fetches me ; "
and here the worthy Cap'n deftly and steadily
pulled up his line with a silver-bellied tomcod
wriggling on his hook. He tenderly cared for
his prey and added : "They do say the gal
takes it ruther hard." He looked at the schoolmaster with an interrogation point in his kindly
gray eyes.

"I do not know as to that," replied Mr.
Woods, " but sometimes when I take my walks
down on Dyce's Head, I observe Pansy sitting
on the rocks and looking with peculiar wistful-
ness out to sea. Perhaps she hopes that David
will come sailing back, some day."

"He ! he ! he !" cackled the Cap'n. "She's
longin' fer him to come back arter she g'in him
the sack, is she ? Wal, all I know is thet my
old woman, she sez thet Nance left Marm Skinner's and took a place down to the lighthouse,
so's to be there on the Head where she could
watch for the Whisper when she comes a-sailin'
in. Wal, the Whisper wont never come a-sailin' in ; ye can jest bet yer boots on that."

" Is it true that Pansy has softened her ways and put on some of the graces of womanhood since the Whisper sailed off on her protracted cruise?" asked the school-master, hesitatingly.

" Wal, I don't know about the softenin' part, but my old woman, she's a master-hand at observin' other wimmen folks, Mis' Grindle is," said the Cap'n with a glow of honest pride, " she says as how the gal's reely quite prinked up. Parts her hair in the middle, 'n' she's got real nice hair now that she's tendin' to it ; 'n my old woman, she sez she's seen Nance wearin' a bow o' red ribbin on her buzzum of'n'; 'n' they do tell she's took to wearin' a bunnit, regular. Gosh all hemlock ! school-master ! Don't you see you've got another bite?"

When Cap'n Grindle went home to his supper, that afternoon, he said to Mrs. Grindle, holding up his string of fish, " Nice mess o' tomcods, Calline, aint it? That ere gawk of a school-master sot 'longside o' me on the wharf, gammin' 'bout Dave Booden 'n Nance Pegg, and got so consarned obligatious 'bout it that he never hauled in ary fish—'cept one sculpin. Queer dick, he is."

Mrs. Grindle regarded her husband with as much asperity as her broad and gentle face was capable of and said: "I sh'd think you two

men could find som'thin' better to do than set
on the edge of the wharf gossipin' about gals
and fellers. Ez for that Pegg gal, she's fell
away awful sence Dave wuz lost. Leastways, I
s'pose he's lost. She's a mere shadder to what
she wuz. But she's a trollop, that's what she
is—a trollop! Ef it hadn't b'en for her, Dave
Booden, who wuz a likely young feller ez ever
drawed the breath of life, would be 'live and
well to-day. Now hurry up, Cap'n, and clean
them fish 'fore supper. A trollop, that's what
she is, pore thing ! ''

All this happened and was said years and
years ago. The loss of the Whisper and her
lonely skipper is remembered only by the elderly folk of Fairport. But the summer visitor,
sauntering among the rocks of rocky pastures of
'' Perkins's Back '' and Dyce's Head, sometimes notes the gaunt, bent form of an old woman who, making her way painfully to a granite
bowlder that overhangs the bluffs, turns her
face, wrinkled with age and whitened and refined by sorrow, seaward from where she sits.
That is Pansy Pegg, with her eyes fixed on the
shining waves, her withered hand at her ear, as
if she expected to hear some whisper from the
sea.

The Apparition of Jo Murch

THE APPARITION OF JO MURCH

IT is no exaggeration to say that Jotham Murch was the worst boy in Old Man Potter's school. It was a town school, and the school committee of the selectmen were often at their wits' end to provide ways and means for the government of the unruly sons of fishermen —boys who had no paternal discipline at home, as their fathers were usually at sea nine months in the year. There was Bob Weeks, for example, whose mother was such a termagant that her husband used to say that fishing on the Grand Banks was "comfortabler than stayin' to home." But even Mrs. Weeks could not wholly beat the spirit of mischief out of Bob, who put red pepper on the school stove, nailed down the lid of the master's desk, interposed with his fists whenever Old Man Potter attempted to ferule a particularly small boy, smoked a tobacco pipe under his own desk, and did many other perverse and mischievous things. Then there was Bill Bridges,

49

who set fire to the school-house ; and Sam Snowman, who stole the master's thermometer, and
whose mother restored it with the tearful remark
that she didn't see '' what possessed Sam to run
off with that air pesky moniment.'' It is not
necessary that I should tell of Joe Triford, who
made squirt-guns of the hollow metal pen-handles
which were in vogue in those days, and who was
a mysterious squirter of ink for four days before
he was found out and handsomely '' rope's-ended '' on his bare legs by the enraged master.
Most of these boys, and others like them, had
been to sea at least one voyage, or had had one
season's experience in fishing off St. George's,
Bay Chaleur, or on the Grand Banks. It is
said that the merchant marine and the United
States Navy draw, or used to draw, their best
men from the ranks of these hardy New England
fishermen. Perhaps so. But in my youth, at
least, no more rough, quarrelsome, and thoroughly heathenish young fellows ever infested
a Christian community than were the majority
of the fishermen's sons around Penobscot Bay.

Still, I will say that Jotham Murch was the
worst boy in the master's school of Fairport.
He was a fighter. He '' sarced '' the big boys
and then kept out of their way ; but the little
boys and he were constantly fighting. He and

I were of the same age and never came to blows but once, and that was when I had interfered in behalf of his younger brother Abe, whom Jotham was pounding to a jelly. Even at this remote period, I record with mortification the fact that I got one of the worst " lickings " that a boy ever had ; but I am also proud to say that Jo emerged from the conflict in a state of raggedness and ruin that was startling to see. The remnants of his shirt, I remember, consisted of a stout unbleached cotton binding buttoned about his neck, and one sleeve, which his forgiving brother had picked up and saved for him. But not for this, not even for being obliged to shake hands with him before the whole school, do I bear Jo Murch any malice.

Before he was fifteen he stole seven shillings and sixpence, New England currency, from his grandmother's light-stand-drawer — a circumstance which gave him the nickname of " Sevenand-six." During that period of adolescence, too, he fixed a big cod-fish hook on the backstay of a ship lying at the wharf, in such a manner that when a poor little chap, whom he had seduced into climbing into the main-top, attempted to escape by the usual way, he was cruelly caught by the leg. He blocked up the mouth of Fred Tilden's rabbit-warren and then deliberately stoned to death four of his white rabbits. As for tying kettles to dogs' tails, bringing cats surreptitiously into the school-room, loading sticks of wood for the school-house stove with powder, "telling on" scholars who played truant, mutilating the books of his enemies, and borrowing books which he never returned —Jo stood at the head of delinquents charged with such offences. He organized and commanded expeditions to plunder the scanty apple-orchards of Fairport; and once he and three other kindred spirits subsisted four days and three nights in the depths of the spruce thickets of the Blockhouse pasture on green corn, turnips, and chickens ravished from the Light-house farm. It should be added that as a liar he was fertile, picturesque, and unconscionable.

At the age of seventeen Jo disappeared from Fairport, having gone to sea with his father, who commanded a square-rigged brig, famous in those coasts for flying at her fore a burgee with "George W. Murch" on it in large letters. Jotham shipped as cabin-boy, was regularly "rope's-ended" by his father, and, smarting with pain and panting for larger liberty, he deserted the square-rigged brig in the port of Surinam. From Havana, about six months afterward, he wrote to his mother for money to pay his passage home. That indulgent parent sent the required sum, but Jo did not return to Fairport. Years went by, and only at long intervals were there any tidings of him. At last he was definitely heard of as being engaged with a thrifty ex-citizen of Fairport, a timber dealer, in Pascagoula, Fla. It was understood that Jo had sowed his wild oats and was trying to save money for his mother; his father, in the meantime, had been lost in a gale which wrecked the square-rigged brig off the coast of Africa. Jo gradually worked his way north, the climate of Florida not agreeing with him; and when he was about twenty-two years old he established himself in the produce and commission business in Boston. His career there was brief. After a few weeks, he absconded with the proceeds of his sales, leaving consignors and shippers nothing but an empty store and a small lot of unpaid-for counting-room furniture by way of indemnity. Meantime, I had left Fairport, and only when I returned on my summer vacations did vague rumors of Jotham's changeful adventures reach me.

Years slipped away, and now and then, like a reminiscence out of a very distant past, would come a report of Jo Murch's being seen or heard from in some foreign land. For example, my big brother Jack, who had then just risen to the command of a fine ship, was lying at Port Mahon, island of Malta, when he heard an altercation at the door of his cabin. Stepping out to see what was the matter, he found a very ragged and dirty man trying to convince the steward that he knew the captain.

"There, now," cried he, as my brother appeared, "that's Captain Rivers. Don't you know me, Jack?"

It was Jo Murch. The steward desisted from his purpose of putting the man over the side of the ship, and gave him up to the captain with obvious surprise.

Jo was forlorn and miserable. But his usual good spirits and impudence had not deserted him. He was at Port Mahon, he said, waiting the arrival of a rich cargo of goods from somewhere. The winds had been contrary; the ship was nineteen days overdue; his expenses were heavy; he had seen Jack's ship reported, and would Jack favor him with a loan of five dollars until the Antigone came in? She must be in soon with this wind, and her cargo was insured for three hundred thousand dollars.

"I'll *give* you the five dollars," said plain-spoken Jack, "for you know you don't intend to pay me, and you know you never will. But

I don't mind giving you five dollars, just for the sake of old times. I would do that for any Fairport boy that I went to school with, if I found him in foreign parts and low down as you seem to be."

Jo accepted the rebuke with great cheerfulness, and protested that he would pay "when his ship came in." Of course that mythical craft never sailed into Port Mahon, nor did Jack lay his eyes on Jotham while he stayed there. Jack was fated to meet Jo once more, many years afterward, during the late civil war. His ship was then lying at Liverpool, embargoed on account of being partly owned by persons living in New Orleans and presumably rebel, as that city was then closed against Union arms and authorities. Jack chafed under this long and unprofitable confinement ; but, though his ship was supposed to be rebel property, he was a furious Union man. He would defend the ship with his life, but he abhorred a rebel.

One day, after a year of idle waiting had passed, who should come on board but Jo Murch. During this long interval his adventures had been various. He had commanded a Russian transport during the Crimean war. He had engaged in trading along the coast of South America. He had done a large business in smuggling cigars from Cuba to Key West, and his present business in Liverpool was to buy a cargo of goods to run the blockade of Savannah. My brother, to use the common phrase, '' opened on him'' for being a rebel and a renegade—a Northern man honestly brought up in Fairport, and now upholding secession and running the blockade ! It was disgraceful, so Jack said.

Jotham was not the man he was at Port Mahon, seven years before. He was now flush of money, well dressed, and prosperous. He not only defended himself, but upbraided Jack in the most abusive terms. The South was right, and it was just such chicken-hearted chaps as Jack (who was tied up with a rebel ownership) who were responsible for the injustice done to Southern people. Jack could not answer this somewhat inconsistent tirade, but he would hear no treason on his ship. If Jo did not '' cork up '' he would fire him out into the dock. Jo did not '' cork up.'' On the contrary, he talked on excitedly about the wrongs of the South, until Jack, who is a tremendous fellow, seized Jo by the collar and the ampler part of his trousers and deliberately threw him overboard. There was a great disturbance, of course ; but Jo escaped with a ducking, while my brother was hauled up before a magistrate and fined ten pounds, which he paid with satisfaction, grimly remarking that it was worth the money.

Nothing more direct than this had reached me from Jotham. He was reputed to have made several millions by his operations during the war, but when peace returned he did not come home with it to enjoy his gains. He settled in Havana, it was said, and married the widow of a sugar-planter. Perhaps it was the necessity of furnishing labor for his sugar plantations which drove him into his next venture; for, not long after this, we heard of his being in the slave-trade off the coast of Africa. This was too horrible for belief, and I could not, somehow, connect even the rapscallion who had been my seat-mate in the Fairport school so long ago, with the slave-trade. But the story came very straight, and, as if to make it certain, there was a later report that Jotham Murch, formerly of Fairport, Me., was hanged in Portsmouth harbor, England, for piracy, otherwise slave-trading. That, at last, seemed to finish Jo Murch.

In the hot summer of 1872, I went one night to my work in the office of the *Morning Clarion.* Mounting to the fifth story of the ricketty, stived building, I stood in the narrow doorway of the editorial rooms, dripping with perspiration and trying to recover my spent breath. From the dark nook where I stood I saw my associates and subordinates grouped about a strange-looking old man. He sat at my desk, with his feet —which were covered with shabby shoes—resting on my writing-pad. His head was quite bald, save for a few wisps of hay-colored hair which fringed its lower edge, like a forgotten aftermath on the margin of a meadow. His nose was flat, and destitute of a bridge. He wore shiny black trousers and a colorless linen duster.

About this ancient mariner—for such he seemed to be—the young gentlemen of the office hung with manifest delight. The stranger was telling them a story. To my amazement, it was a tolerably faithful narrative of a disreputable adventure in which I had been engaged during my school-days, say thirty years before. Somewhat nettled, as well as bewildered, I emerged from the shadow and advanced into the gas-lighted room. One of the listeners said to the ancient mariner, "This is Mr. Rivers," whereupon they all scattered to their several desks. The ancient mariner took down his feet, and, with a gesture of surprise, said:

"Why, Bill! How are you?"

He made as if he would seize me by the hand, but I coldly drew back with :

" I can't say that I know you."

The forlorn-looking old man, whom I now saw was also nearly toothless, cried, with glee :

" I thought you wouldn't know me !   Why, I'm Jo Murch ! "

If the spirit of my grandfather, whose gravestone in Fairport burying-ground was mossy when I was a school-boy, had risen through the floor of the *Morning Clarion* office, I could not have been more astonished.

In my surprise, I blurted out my instant thought—" Jo Murch ?   Why, I thought you were hanged in Portsmouth harbor ! "

" Oh, no," said Jo, blithely, " that was another feller.   Just like you newspapers— always getting things wrong end first ! "

" Well, Jo, I'm glad to see you anyway." And I trust that the recording angel dropped a tear of pity for poor Jo, as he wrote down this charitable falsehood.   I was not glad to see this strange apparition.   Jo Murch was a handsome, bright-eyed young fellow, a favorite with the girls, and a lady-killer when he came to man's estate.   This aged person did not have Jo Murch's Roman nose, nor his fresh complexion, nor his upright carriage and elastic tread.   He was bald, bent, seamed, brown, and broken-nosed.

" I never should have known you, Jo."

" No, dare say not ; but *you* are as handsome and rosy and well fed as ever—eh, you fat rascal ! "   And he punched me in the stomach with a skinny finger.   " I—well—*I* have had adventures since you licked me so like tarnation at Old Man Potter's school."

The associate editors giggled at their desks, and the foreign news editor interrupted us to ask if he should set Gladstone's speech in minion, leaded, with a pica head, or run it up solid, with a brevier italic.

Jo's stormy and checkered career as a blockade-runner, slave-trader, smuggler, and foreign mercenary, flitted mistily through my mind, as I directed Gladstone to be set in minion, leaded, with a brevier italic head and minion cap under.

Jo cocked his head on one side, with a parrot-like leer, and remarked :

" Old man Potter would be mightily tickled to see you bossing Gladstone's speech.   Don't you remember that time the old man tore your satinet trousers off of you, trying to get at a good place to wallop you with his ferule ? "

" Do ye moind if I set it in nonpareel ?   I

fancy it would be shuparior," interrupted the foreign editor. And there was another slight snicker of laughter around the office.

" You see, Jo, I'm pretty busy at this time of night. Come up to my lodgings to-morrow, and we will talk over old times." And Jotham went away with a promise to see me in Van Tassell Place, next day, between two and four in the afternoon.

" That gentleman seems to have been a great traveller," remarked one of my associates.

" Yes, and if you have any copy ready for to-morrow morning's paper, suppose you rush it upstairs."

And so the weary burden of the night was taken up again, and Jo Murch faded out of mind.

Next day, as the yellow heat rained into the cracks of my closed blinds, in Van Tassel Place, the housemaid knocked on the door, opened it, and said : " A quare-lookin' gintleman is axin for yez at the fut of the shtair."

With that, Jo's wrinkled and yellow face appeared over her shoulder, and he said :

" And it's meself, ye purty dear, that's just forninst yez."

The indignant girl darted a flash of scorn at the intruder, let him into the room, shut the door with a bang of disapproval, and clattered out of sight, but not until Jo had put his head over the banisters and cried :

" Fetch us up a pitcher of good cold ice-water, there's a nice girl. It's hotter than blue blazes to-day."

Jo looked even more seedy and worn in the gay beams of garish day than in the gaslight. As I regarded him attentively, it was impossible to discover a trace of the boy who had sat in the same seat with me in Sunday-school and at Old Man Potter's. He was curiously bent in the back, his nose was abnormal in shape, and even his eye had a queer squint which was not so before. But there was no mistaking the air of easy impudence with which he tossed on the table a small wooden box which he carried, stripped off his linen duster, kicked his broken shoes into a corner, and threw himself on the sofa with the manifest intention of taking things easy.

" Hand me that fan, will you, Bill ? Thanks ; this is the hottest of the hot, I guess ; hotter than old Mary Ann Hot. I have not seen such a day outside of Timbuctoo. I was there in '51. Ever in Timbuctoo ? No ? Well, it's hotter than New York."

" How long have you been in New York,

and where were you from when you came here, Jo?"

"Oh, don't ask me now. It's too long a yarn. Wait till I get cool. By the way, have you any objection to my peeling off my pants? I could cool quicker in my drawers. Blame these black cassimeres, anyhow. I have to wear 'em this hot weather by the advice of my doctor. Legs, you know"—and here Jo struggled with his trousers—"legs must be protected at all hazards. I had a fever when I was in Leghorn. By the way, have you got a good cigar? I've got some first-chop down to my hotel; smuggled 'em myself, and I ought to know."

Jo ensconced himself again on the sofa, half undressed, with a fragrant cigar in his lips, stretched at full length, and with his indescribable legs, which bore signs of a Leghorn fever, comfortably crossed.

"Great thing, Bill, this linen spread on a sofa in summer, and such summers as they do have in New York! By the way, how do you suppose I found out where you were?"

"I give it up," somewhat ruefully.

"Well, I saw a story of yours in the *Picknickers' Magazine*. It had several Fairport names in it, likewise some reminiscences of

Fairport school-days. Oh, don't you remember that time Alf Martin and I drove the skunk into Miss Dawson's school? My! how those girls did scud! I can see Almira Dawson now, hitching up her skirts and making for the tall grass. Let me see, where was I? Mozambique? Oh, no! I was telling how I found you. Well, I went to the office of the *Picknickers'* ; stiff lot they are. They wouldn't tell where I could find you. Told 'em I was an old friend and all that sort of thing, you know; no go; could only find that you lived in New York. So I went to the ' City Directory,' looked among the R's ; not many Riverses ; found you were in the *Clarion* office, and here I am—just as easy.''

Jo at once made himself very much at home ; helped himself to cigars from a box on the table ; inquired if I had anything to drink ; and, when he had stretched himself again on the sofa, with a fresh cigar in his lips and a big glass of ginger-ale and ice within easy reach, he sighed comfortably, and said that this was '' really very tidy.''

'' Let me see—where was I ? '' murmured Jo, between puffs of his cigar. '' Oh, I told you I would tell you where I had been. Dear, dear me, to think that you and I should meet again after so many years! Say, Bill, don't you remember that time when we had that fight down to the Back Cove, how I closed up one of your eyes with blue clay when we were making marbles on the shore? Golly! what a walloping you gave me!"

"Beg pardon, Jo, 'twas I who got the walloping; but I do remember that I tore your clothes all off of you."

"So you did—so you did, Bill; and I remember that when I went home that afternoon I had to stand with my back against the fence when I met some of the girls, I was tore so awfully behind." And Joe kicked up his crooked legs and laughed so uproariously that the street-boys passing by caught the strain, and ran away ha-haing with a mocking chorus. Jo heard it, and suddenly growing grave, said:

"How much worse the boys are now than they used to be when we were boys! Impudent, idle, thievish vagabonds! I suppose the boys of the present generation are the worst that ever were. By the way," he continued, with animation, "were you a Union man during the war?"

"Certainly I was."

"So I supposed. Your brother Jack was a hell-roaring Yank. Why, I met him in Liverpool, where he was tied up with a part-rebel ownership, and when we ventured on a little discussion about the war, he threatened to chuck me overboard if I didn't cork up."

"He says he did throw you overboard," said I.

"He says so!" screamed Jo, sitting up on end. "He says so! Well, I never!—Well, perhaps he did; I really don't recollect, it was so long ago." And Jo calmly settled back again.

"What were you doing in Liverpool during the war?" I inquired.

"Oh, yes, I must tell you about that. You see, I was United States Consul at Jacmel, West Indies, when the war broke out. My sympathies were with the South, and so I went into blockade-running. My position gave me lots of advantage over the other fellows, and we did a great business. Our vessels used to run into Jacmel with a full cargo, and wait for a good time when there was no moon and we knew where the Yankee cruisers were. Then we would run into Charleston, Savannah, Mobile, or wherever we could do best."

"You must have had a big capital to operate with, Jo."

"I should say so. Why, our books used to

show a business of five million a year. And then the fun! Why, hunting bears on Great Mountain was nothing to it. Don't you remember how you and I and Dave Patchin got chased by a bear, and we had nothing but a single-barrelled gun between us? But in blockade-running you are chased by a man-of-war that may blow you to kingdom come with one shot, whereas a bear — give me a light, will you? Thanks. Well, as I was saying, being United States Consul, I got the hang of the thing, and was just coining money. My share was five hundred thousand dollars, all in good gold coin. Then your confounded mean old government got after me. One day a sharp-faced Yankee from Rhode Island came into my office, just as I was lying back after settling up my profits of the last cruise. He said that he had been appointed to take my place. Reports of 'irregularities' had reached the State Department, he said. 'Irregularities!' Wasn't that good? I showed fight, of course, but he showed his papers and I had to surrender. And, come to think of it, it wasn't just the thing, you see, for a United States Consul to be engaged in running the blockade, was it?"

"I should say that it wasn't."

"No, of course not; but then you see I was

devoted to the South, and the end justifies the
means, you know, and all that sort of thing."

"Especially when you are making half a
million a year," I interposed.

"Yes," said Jo, with a sigh, "but that all
went."

"All went? Did you lose it, after all?"

"Every stiver of it. After I was cheated
out of my consulship I went on one or two
voyages myself. It was on my first to
Liverpool for a cargo that I fell in with Jack,
when he threw me — I mean threatened to
throw me—into the dock. On my second
voyage into Charleston I was chased by the
Osceola and the Kittywink, two United States
gun-boats. We had an assorted cargo, worth
four hundred thousand dollars. Ours was a
side-wheel steamer, eighteen knots an hour,
painted lead color, paddle-wheels twenty-five
feet in diameter; greased lightning was nothing
to her for speed. I was on the bridge when
the Osceola hove in sight, just coming around
a black point of rocks on the port bow. I
laughed, for I knew the Osceola—an old tub,
built in East Boston; never made more than
ten knots an hour. So we streaked it ahead,
the Yankee just about three points on our port
bow, and plunging ahead as if she would cut us

off. We left her just as easy as lying, when, all of a sudden, as she had fired a couple of shots, just to show how mad her people were, out runs, from the darkness, another gun-boat! It was the Kittywink. Where she came from, the Lord only knows. I had Seth Grindle with me. You remember Seth? The same fellow that used to steal apples and hide them in the fire-buckets in the school-house when we went to Cynthy Ann Rogers's school. Well says I to Seth, ' Seth, if that's the Kittywink, we are done for.' But Seth was clear grit. Says he, ' We may have to throw some of the cargo overboard, but we will never be taken alive.' So I told him to get the hatches open and everything ready to throw over the cargo, and we cracked on all steam.''

" It must have been exciting.''

" Exciting! I should say so. You should have seen that vessel of ours fly. And abeam of us, about two miles and a quarter away, the Yankee gun-boat darted like a flash. Tell you what! she was a regular screamer. She bore down on us, never firing a gun, still as death, without so much as a light to be seen on board. We had a straight line; the Yankee had a long, oblique one. But he was light, and we had a heavy cargo. The little Adger just fairly trembled as her tremendous wheels went round and round. The Kittywink seemed to gain on us: she did gain on us. Then she fired a round shot across our bow, as a polite invitation to heave to. Of course we hove to! Seventy cases of Enfield rifles, the property of the Confederacy, went overboard. Old Sumter hove in sight, the stars and bars fluttering from its ruined wall. The gun-boat gained on us, when —'bang! bang!' went a couple of guns from Sumter. The Lord was kind to the Confederacy that night; for in three minutes more we were under the guns of the fort. We slackened steam, gave three cheers, and leisurely paddled up to the city, the Yankee going off as mad as a wet hen, I've no doubt."

"So that was not the time you lost your ill-gotten millions?"

"Ill-gotten millions! Well, I like that; some folks are so prejudiced! No, that wasn't the time, but it *was*, for all that. You see I was taken down with the infernal malarial fever they have at Charleston; couldn't go back on the Adger when she returned, as she did soon. Perhaps it was just as well, for she was captured by the Kittywink—bad 'cess to her— and was carried off as a prize to Fortress Monroe. I saw her after the peace, turned into

a pleasure-yacht for the Secretary of the Navy
to go junketing around with.   As I was saying,
my sickness prevented my going back for nearly
six months ; and when I got out by the way of
Savannah and Nassau, my precious partners
had vamosed the ranch.   They had left Jacmel
with every dollar of company funds, and all I
had was a bill of exchange on London for five
hundred pounds.   I never saw one of those
partners afterward, except Hernandez, a big
Spanish thief.   I met him in Homburg two
years ago, playing the part of croupier at one of
the gambling tables. ' Why,' says I, with a
jump, ' it's Hernandez, the thief ! '   He never
so much as winked, but went right on with his
everlasting ' Faty voo le joo, Messers.'   But it
was Hernandez.''

Jo lighted another cigar.   Then he went on :
'' By the way, Bill, who do you suppose I met
once in the Crimea ?   Why, Sidney Price !
He was the worst boy at Old Man Potter's
school, I do believe.''

'' Oh, Jo, you do yourself injustice.''

Jo grinned, and replied :

'' The fact is, we all overlooked Sid's fault
because he was a nigger.   Niggers were scarce
in Fairport in our time ; none there but the
Prices and Leather-belly Richardson.''

Here Jo broke into a long laugh, during which he fell into a fit of coughing, rolled off the lounge to the floor, where he lay choking and strangling, much to my alarm. I raised him up and tried the old-fashioned remedy of clapping him on the back. As soon as he recovered his speech, he said, angrily:

"Don't do that! You are slapping me on my old wound."

"Your old wound, Jo?" I said. "How should I know you had any?"

"Yes, that's where a Spanish devil of a count ran me through with a small-sword. I fought a duel with the dirty beggar in Seville. Every time I catch a cold it settles on my lungs, where the darned garlic-eater's toad-sticker went through. That's what makes me cough so."

"What was the duel about, Jo?"

"About a woman, of course. What is any duel about?" replied Jo, sitting up on the floor and relighting his cigar with a match which he had carefully scratched on the rosewood framework of my sofa.

"Let me see, where was I?" asked Jo, as he scrambled back to his seat. "Oh, we were talking about old Rich. Don't you remember how we used to yell 'Leather-belly! Leather-belly Richardson!' at him from behind a corner? How mad he used to get! He would drop his saw and saw-horse and go for us. I recollect how he caught you once and nearly pounded the life out of you until 'Libby and Snelgro' came along. You remember we used to call Charley Grindle 'Libby and Snelgro,' because he used to tell that awful murder story about Libby and Snelgro to us boys. Dear me! I remember one night when we were scooting through the graveyard after we had been stealing apples out of Mark Hatch's orchard, and Charley Grindle came along and made us sit down on Captain Skinner's gravestone while he told us that confounded story over again. That was the night Jake Norton broke his front tooth out trying to bite through an apple with a pebble punched into it. Let me see, where was I?"

"You were talking about old Richardson, and meeting Sidney Price in the Crimea. What were you doing in the Crimea, Jo?"

"Yes, yes, so I was. Dear me! how these boyish reminiscences do come over a feller once in a while. Why, one time when I was in Norway, where I was after a cargo of lumber —but let me tell you about Sid Price. I had command of a French transport in the Crimean

War, La Magicienne, they called her—a perfect old tub, about the size of the William and Sally that old Snowman used to sail out of Fairport. You remember old Snowman? He had a one-eyed boy. But, as I was saying, I was discharging a cargo of shells and fixed ammunition at Kostenika, a little one-horse port in the Crimea. The Allies were investing Sevastopol, and the Turks were in a devil of a hurry for the French to come up. The French, you know, were always behindhand with their ammunition——''

"No, I didn't know that," I interrupted.

"Well, they were, and on this occasion a big swell-headed Turk, a bashaw of some kind, came off to the barque with a remonstrance or something written in first-rate Turkish, but not a word of which could I understand. Says I, after turning the paper upside down and t'other side up : ' You go see Admiral. He's boss. I no sabe this manifest, or whatever the devil it is. Go to Admiral. Sabe?' The Turkey feller looked at me mighty hard, and says he to me : ' Jo Murch, as sure's I'm a livin' sinner ! ' Says I to him, says I, ' Leather-belly ! ' It was Porter Richardson's grandson, Sid Price.''

"Oh, come now, Jo, that's an old story,

74

fixed over. Ever so many men have told that of their old comrades,'' I remonstrated.

Jo put on an injured air and declared that it was the truth. Moreover, he added that Sidney Price had been cast away on the coast of Tripoli, in the bark Antioch, of Fairport, that he had been sold into slavery, then taken to Pera, where he saved the life of a son of the Sultan by diving into the Bosphorus where the young man was drowning in a leisurely manner, after falling from a passing craft. Once free, Jo continued, the young negro advanced very rapidly in favor with the big-wigs, and, being about half white, passed for a Turk.

'' And he reflected great credit on the Fairport town school,'' added Jo, '' although I never shall forget how he used invariably to bound the kingdom of Portugal by Norway and Sweden, wiping out half of the map of Europe at one lick. And, by the way, don't you suppose your landlady would send you up a bite of something to eat if you were to ring for it— just a snack, you know? I'm devilish hungry. Hot weather always makes me hungry —does some folks, you know. I'm peculiar about that.''

I rang the bell, and Bridget, opening the door, caught one glimpse of Jo, half undressed, with his heels in the air, as he lay on the sofa. She gave a little shriek with a suppressed giggle in it, and clapped the door to. Going out, I found her blushing over the banisters.

" The likes of that ! " she said, severely.

Giving the needed orders, I went into the room and found Jo laughing heartily.

" Just like those Irish girls ! They put on more frills — why, when I was in London once——"

But I never heard the rest of the story, for Jo's eye catching sight of a water-color sketch on the wall, he rose hastily, and shuffling across the floor, gazed at it a moment in silence, and exclaimed :

" Why, that's San José de Guatemala, by the living jingo ! "

" Certainly," said I. " What of it, Jo ? "

" Oh, nothing," said he, throwing himself down again on the sofa. " Nothing. When were you there——for I suppose you sketched that yourself ? "

" Yes ; I was there in 1867, on my way to Panama from San Francisco, in a coasting vessel."

" Well, I was there in '66. Don't you remember that invasion they had from San Salvador that year ? Oh, my eye ! such a fight

I saw!" And Jo rolled back and laughed until he coughed again.

"You see," he continued, "there was first a revolution—one of those one-horse revolutions, such as they get up in the Central American States any day for the amusement of visitors. See this nose?" asked Jo, sitting up and laying his finger on that organ. "Well, this is how it came about. One bright morning while I was in Chicoroso—that little town which, you remember, is half-way between San José and the border of San Salvador—I was lying in bed, wondering why Dolores did not bring my chocolate. Mine was a little adobe hut, with an oiled-paper window on the left of the bed, about three feet away, and the adobe wall close on the right. I was flat on my back, watching the rats running over the cloth lining of the ceiling overhead. Suddenly I heard muskets popping away outside, as if in the plaza, as they call the hole in the middle of the village where they dump their rubbish. 'Aha! a revolution!' thinks I to myself. I began to speculate whether it would be possible for me to make anything out of it, for I had bills of credit on Dreyfus & Co. for two hundred and fifty thousand reals, and could have bought up the whole contemptible concern if there was anything in it.

"While I was a-thinking, 'bang!' came a musket-ball through the window, crashed through the bridge of my nose—half an inch lower, and it would have been good-by, Jo Murch!—and buried itself in the adobe wall. Here it is, you see; picked it out afterward; I keep it for luck."

And Jo showed me a battered lump of lead, bright with the constant friction which it had received by being carried in his pocket.

"A narrow escape for you, Jo," I said, handling the flattened bullet. "Was it much of a revolution?"

"No; I was the only man wounded. The general-in-chief of the insurgents, a big, bare-footed greaser, with a ragged straw hat and no clothes worth mentioning, was captured by the government ragamuffins in the first rush. The 'insurgents,' as they called them, made a raid on the shop of a German Jew, the only foreign trader in the place, and when both contending armies had divided the plunder, the revolution simmered down. By the way, that trader's name was Snelgro. Queer, wasn't it? Do you remember whether Snelgro killed Libby, or was it Libby who killed Snelgro, down in Fairport, years and years ago? Hokey! I just remember how I and you met Charlie

Grindle one day when we were out hunting squirrels with bows and arrows, and how we sat down on a flat rock in Hatch's back pasture, while he told us over again the whole story about how Libby killed Snelgro, or Snelgro killed Libby, I've forgotten which it was ; and when he got through he said, lifting up his own, ' And that's the gun he killed him with ! ' Golly ! how it scared me ! I was younger then than I am now. That was the second time he told us that yarn. But I believe he lied. He was an awful liar, Charley Grindle was."

Somehow, Jo's reminiscences of our boyhood were not so entertaining to me as those of his later adventures. I gently led him back to Guatemala.

" Oh, yes ! Well, you see, that is how my beautiful nose got damaged. 'Tisn't so bad, though, do you think ? " And Jo went to the mirror, turned around so that the light might not spare his defective nose, smirked at himself, and added : " Well, anyhow, I've been married twice since that damage was done, and that's more than a good many handsomer fellows can say."

" Why didn't you bring a bill of damages against the government, Jo ? "

" Damages! government!" echoed Jo, with
disdain. "Why, you might as well sue a beggar as to sue one of them Central American
governments. There never is any government;
and as for trade, why, a canoe-load of red peppers would swamp the market any day. Speak-
ing of peppers, did I show you my sewing-
machine? Here it is," and going to the table,
Jo opened the little case which I had observed
in his hand when he came in. It contained a
little polished brass machine, with two or three
wheels and pinions, and a needle.

"Look at her! ain't she a beauty? There's
cords of money in that. You can't begin to
think of the amount of time and thought and
money I've put into it. It does the work of one
of those rip-tearing, clumsy things of Grover
& Wilson, and in half the time, twice as
good, no fuss, no breakage, or the money re-
funded. Any child can work it, takes up only
seven and a half cubic inches, and costs only
nine dollars. Say, old fellow, you ought to
buy one of 'em for your Aunt Priscilla, just for
a toy curiosity, you know. It costs nothing,
but, seeing it's you, I'll let you have it for the
net price, seven dollars, which is only thirty-
three per cent. above cost at first hands. Want
one?"

I told Jo that my Aunt Priscilla hated sewing-machines, and could not abide the sight of anything that saved labor.

"Well," said Jo, with a sigh, "I was carrying this up to One Hundred and Sixty-ninth Street, where I have a large order pending, and it's so bloody hot to-day that I thought I would leave it on you and go up there some other day. Why, while I was getting up this machine, do you know that Grimshaw, Bagshaw, & Bradshaw, the great sewing-machine monopolists, actually bribed my clerks and stole my plans and models? Oh, I was telling you about that invasion of Guatemala, wasn't I now? By the way, these are darn bad cigars. Thanks! this does look better. Let me send you a box of Pumariegas, smuggled, you know. But we Yanks do enjoy a thing more for its being a leetle, just a leetle, unlawful, don't we?"

Jo settled himself comfortably and took up the thread of his discourse. Guatemala, he said, had been invaded from San Salvador, and both "armies," consisting of about fifty men each, had encamped on opposite sides of the little town of Chicoroso, just at night-fall. During the night one of the Guatemalan sentries accidentally discharged his musket. Instantly both camps were in an uproar and the firing was incessant. In the confusion each party imagined itself attacked, and each promptly turned and ran. When morning broke, the astonished citizens of Chicoroso found themselves without defenders or assailants. Both armies had run away during the night.

" But you should have seen the reception," continued Jo. " When the victorious army of Guatemala returned to the capital, the President went out to meet them with a guard of honor— sixteen tatterdemalions with bits of red flannel on their shoulders by way of uniform. The only casualty in the victorious army was one fellow who had sprained his ankle by being chucked off of a bucking mule. He wanted to get home to his wife, but they put him on a litter and covered him over with the Guatemala flag, while the President made a speech congratulating the brave defenders of the republic on their glorious victory, and complimenting them for their prowess. You should have seen the poor devil with the sprained ankle. Two or three times he would try to escape, groaning and swearing horribly. But his comrades held him on the litter and corked him up by cramming the flag into his mouth, while the President went on about their ' heroic wounded.' Oh, it was as funny as a rag."

"Well, Jo, some of our own politicians organize 'receptions' and parades on the same plan, you know. People are pretty much alike, wherever you find them."

"That's so! that's so!" broke in Jo, who excitedly took another cigar as he went on to state the case. "Why, Bill, I've seen pretty much all there is worth seeing in this world; been everywhere, seen all races, and there's just two things that you can set down as fixed facts. In the first place, this is a dreadful small world. When you've been round the globe once or twice, it's surprising how little it seems. Why, when I was a boy, it was farther from Fairport to Boston, to me, than it is around the world now. The other thing is, that folks are pretty much of a muchness, wherever you find 'em. There's philosophy for you, Bill; but I know. I've been there."

"You mean to say that human nature is the same in all countries and under all conditions?"

"Not only that, but folks are folks, whether you find 'em in Kamschatka or under the equator. I remember how I once laid under a babo-tree in Senegambia and watched the little niggers at play—native Africans, understand, not the American improved patent nigger, but the original article. I swear to you, Bill, those young Africans were playing the same games we used to play on the common in Fairport, years and years ago. There was ' High-spy,' ' Long-come-on,' ' Horam-a-goram,' and all the rest ; and they had a ball-game just like our old round-ball,—not the high-falutin base-ball they play in this country. Base-ball hadn't been intro-duced into Senegambia when I was there," Jo added, with a chuckle.

" What were you doing on the coast of Afri-ca, Jo?"

" Carrying passengers," replied my visitor, with a quiet laugh.

" Was the passenger traffic profitable?" I asked. I suddenly remembered Jo's bad repu-tation as a slave-trader.

" Just pass me that bottle, and I'll give you an example. It's a long story," and here Jo took a long drink, leaned over the sofa and care-fully tucked the bottle underneath, settled him-self comfortably, and began :

" I was commanding the Paul Jones, a square-rigged brig, Baltimore built, and originally as fast as chain-lightning, but rather dull then. We had three hundred and sixty passengers on board."

" Negroes?"

" Niggers. Mostly black passengers on that coast. The third day out of the mouth of the Loando we sighted her Britannic Majesty's ship Gorgon, hull down, but bouncing along with a free wind and all sail set. I knew the old devil the minute we raised her fore-to'-gallan'-s'ls ; knew their cut. I laughed and said to Scotty —Scotty was my first mate, you see, born in Dumfries, and a first-class sailor. ' Scotty,' says I, ' that old tub is a sailer, but the Paul Jones will leave her so far behind, before eight bells, that you will never see that flat to'-gallan'-s'l again. Now, you mind.' And I meant it. It was a stern chase, you see, Bill."

" But why should there be any chase, Jo ? I don't understand."

" Well, you see, on them coasts the Britishers have everything their own way, as it were. They've made a set of laws about carrying passengers which they enforce dreadful particular. I tell you how. They allow so many passengers to the ton ; more than that, when a feller's found with too many passengers on board of them, those meddling British frigates just lay alongside and make things uncomfortable with their blasted laws. Oh, they're just pizen, I tell you. But, as I was saying, I guessed I was all hunky, so we kept right on our course, having crowded on every stitch of canvas the old brig could carry. When just as we were widening the distance between us so that the Gorgon began to sink below the horizon again, we struck a dead calm! You know how the wind flies in them latitudes?—just goes and comes in streaks. Here was the Paul Jones in a sea like a millpond, scarcely a cat's-paw on the surface. And there was the cussed Britisher with a seven-knot breezer coming up hand over hand."

"And your passengers, Jo?"

" That was it. They were first-rate chaps, those passengers. When the danger of our being overhauled first dawned on them, they were so much attached to me that they actually said they'd sooner go overboard than get me into any trouble. Fact! they did. I said that that would be a little too bad. Really, I couldn't ask it of 'em. But matters grew worse very fast; and then, to think of the ingratitude of niggers! Do you believe it! they changed their minds and said they wouldn't go overboard; no, not for no money! What could I do? Of course I got my back up at that, and they walked the plank—the whole kit and caboodle."

" You don't mean to tell me, Jo, that you threw these people overboard?"

"Why, not exactly, you see. They had

agreed to go over peaceably, of their own free will and accord, man-fashion. It was their own offer. I shouldn't ever have thought of it if they hadn't suggested it first. So they went over—for'ard, as they might have been noticed going over the side, and unpleasant remarks might have been made in the frigate. But it was growing dusk, and everything was serene in an hour or two. When the calm struck the Gorgon she was two miles away, and it was almost dark. She kept by us all night, and when old Fuss-and-Feathers, her commander, sent his boat alongside next morning, at daybreak, I showed him my papers, my cargo of palm-oil and ivory — just a little stock, of course, but all regular—and he had nothing much to say."

"So you actually threw those three hundred and sixty negroes overboard, Jo?"

"Oh, no, don't say that. You exaggerate," said Jo, deprecatingly. "I don't think there was so many ; not more than three hundred and fifty odd, I'm sure. Besides, didn't I tell you that they agreed to go of their own free will and accord? *Que voulez-vous ?* as the Frenchman says."

Here Jo picked himself up in a leisurely manner, drew on his trousers, and, looking toward the little box on the table, said :

"So you won't take one of my machines to-day?"

I told him that I really did not want it; whereupon he dressed himself in a slow, musing manner, put on his hat, took his box under his arm, told me that it was like seeing a play to meet me again after so many years, bade me adieu and went out, shutting the door after him.

I was straightening out the linen sofa-cover where he had lain, and reducing the scattered disorder of the room, when the door suddenly reopened and Jo, with a brisk and business-like air, came back.

"Say, Bill," he said, "I find I haven't got any change about me for my car-fare. Came away and left my wallet in my other breeches. Give me a little change now, and I'll drop in on you to-night and pay you."

"All right, Jo," said I. "How much do you want?"

"Oh, I guess a couple of dollars will do."

"But isn't two dollars a good deal for car-fare?" I asked, with sudden surprise.

"Well, you see it's such a deuce of a ways, away up to One Hundred and Fiftieth Street, you know," replied Jo, smiling ruefully.

"Day-day!" said he, cheerily, as he put the bank-note into his pocket. "I'll drop in on you at the *Clarion* office to-night, and bring you a box of those cigars, besides. So glad I've seen you ! "

He went softly down-stairs, opened the street door, looked out into the hot street, now growing yellower in the declining sunlight, looked back at me with a ghastly smile, and closed the door behind him. As I never have seen or heard of him from that day to this, or knew of anybody who saw him after I did, I am not at all certain but what this was the apparition of Jotham Murch, hanged for piracy in Portsmouth harbor.

The Hereditary Barn

THE HEREDITARY BARN

THE old Joslin farm is on the road from Fairport to Penobscot, near the head of the Northern Bay. It is a ragged and hilly piece of upland, yielding good grass, and capable of great possibilities in the way of potatoes. But the Joslins never did stick to farming as a sole means of getting a living. The old-fashioned, gambrel-roofed house, mossy as to roof and dark red as to its front, overlooked the Northern bay; and it was a pretty dull time when at least one coaster could not be seen lazily creeping up to Penobscot with the tide in her favor; or it may have been a hay-sloop that dropped down, equally lazy, with the ebb. And it was part of the domestic economy of the farmers of the Bay, that a goodly share of the winter's provisions should consist of codfish, caught on the Grand Banks by some younger member of the family, or " traded for " by the head of the house with some more adventurous neighbor. The population of the region around the Doshan shore and the head of the Northern Bay is largely amphibious. Fishing, coasting, and kindred seamanlike pursuits fill in the chinks of the dull life of the tillers of the soil.

It is not an inspiring landscape that the eyes of the Joslins were used to look on from the door-stone of their ancient homestead. From the little pinched-up flower garden, where marigolds, hollyhocks, love-lies-bleeding, and China asters disputed the ground with balm, sweet marjoram, and mother-wort, the land sloped steeply off to the bluff overhanging the river. A tidy rail-fence skirted the lower edge of the place, and the Penobscot road, yellow with golden-rod and ox-eyed daisies in autumn, and gullied with heavy rains in spring, crept along under the fence, half-hidden from the house and dangerously near the crumbling bluff of the river-bank.

From the house, overlooking road and bluff, the eye fell on a long and narrow bay, or estuary, of the broader bay of Penobscot. The farther shore was well wooded, and the sombre spruces and firs, never very cheerful, were black and mournful indeed in winter. The waters of the bay were never vexed by many keels, and the few farming settlements on the farther side of the water were so hidden by the woods that one might almost fancy it an untrodden wilderness, if it were not for the glimpses given, here and there, of bits of ploughed land. Beyond the woods that rose upward from the shore was the distant serrated range of the Mount Desert hills, blue and cold in the eastern sky; and farther to the north, the honest face of Blue Hill, rugged and seamy, reposed against the horizon. The picture might have been transferred to canvas, and shown to a northern traveller as a view of a Norwegian fiord, so dark and cold and stern was it.

The red-fronted house looked unwinkingly on the scene from two Lutheran windows in its roof; and an open woodshed, that terminated in a hen-house, stretched itself from the house almost over to a big barn, black with age, but substantial and more suggestive of wealth and comfort than even the old farm-house itself. It was a well-shingled and glass-windowed barn, ample with its hay-mows and stalls for cattle, and affording refuge for colonies of barn-swallows that built their mud-nests under its hospitable eaves. It had a homely look—that time-blackened barn; but far up in the northern gable an eye-shaped aperture for the martens which nested among the rafters within, looked over the waters of the bay with a fixed and sinister stare. Seen from the road, at the height of a summer noon, when all hands were in the fields, and the cat kept house on the sun-drenched window-sill, the place seemed forlorn and lonely. It might have been a lost farm— a farm dropped by accident by some giant peddler passing that way with a load of build-ings and fences for sale.

Very gloomy and poverty-stricken did the Joslin place appear to old man Joslin in the winter of 1807, when, an embargo having been declared by the United States Government, a blight fell on every industry of the New Eng-land seaboard States. There was Elkanah Jos-lin's hay waiting to be sold and shipped; in the cellar were fifty bushels of good, sound po-tatoes that would rot before a customer could be found for them. And even the five shares which Elkanah owned in the John and Eliza were worthless as so much driftwood; and there was the schooner "eating her head off," as the farmer sourly expressed it, in Portland harbor, idle and useless as long as the embargo lasted. Smuggling from the Provinces was the only thriving industry in the time of the em-bargo; but Elkanah Joslin was an uncompro-mising church-member. He would sooner starve than break the law of the land.

" 'Pears to me that there ain't no sort of use tryin' to make a cent, nowadays," said Elkanah, complainingly. He sat down heavily on the blue-painted settle that shut off the draught from the door, and drawing back from the fire his lumbering and leaden feet, gazed at his loosely locked hands, that rested between his knees. " 'Tain't no use," he repeated.

Brisk Marm Joslin, having carefully boxed the ears of young Amzi, who was filching an apple from the wooden bowl she held in her lap, said, as she added one more to the heap of peeled fruit, " Wal, Elkanah, you are the beatenest critter to git diskerriged in no time that I almost ever saw. It's morally sartin that the dimbargo will be declared off airly in the spring. We've got enough in the house to last us through till the frost comes out o' the ground; hogs to kill, a calf comin' in in March, and clothes fit to kerry us through. Land sakes alive! what does the man want? the hull airth?"

Old man Joslin made no reply, except in a long-drawn sigh that seemed to come up laboriously from the very depths of his homespun garments. He looked fixedly at his stubby finger-nails and toil-worn hands, and his watery

blue eyes filled with unaccustomed moisture as
he revolved in his mind the desolateness and
the poverty of his lot.   It was true that he had
enough to eat and drink for himself and his ;
but it irked him to think he had properties
lying idle, deteriorating with disuse, and liable
to perish utterly.   Besides, Jotham, his eldest
and his hope, had come home from Boston with
a hacking cough, and the doctor said that it
looked as if he might go into a decline.   Most
of the Philbricks—Marm Joslin was a Philbrick
—had gone off in declines ; so Elkanah sat and
brooded over his troubles until the short December day was ended, and the twilight fell
quickly around the gambrel-roofed house, investing its sombreness with a yet deeper mel-
ancholy, and leaving all the outer landscape
vague and weird in the ghostliness of the
approaching winter night.

Old Elkanah rose stiffly, resting his horny
hand on the top of the settle to help bring
his rusty frame into a perpendicular.   Saying
"Guess I'll tend to the critters," he shambled
out of the door, and was lost in the shadows of
the barn.   Her bowl of apples pared, Marm
Joslin also rose, but with a quick alertness
strikingly in contrast with the movements of
her husband, wiped her hands, pulled out the

tea-table with a prodigious clatter, and began laying the cloth. But pausing in her work for a moment, before she lighted the whale-oil lamp that stood on the mantel-piece, she went to the window, and watched the drooping form of Elkanah as he plodded toward the barn.

" Poor Elkanah," she sighed to herself; " he don't look like the spry young feller he was forty year ago." Then she paused, as if recalling the memory of the young Elkanah who courted her in Prospect, before the British evacuated Fairport, and while the colonists were not certain whether they were to be citizens of a republic or subjects of a king.

"But he is the beatenest critter," she murmured, impatiently. Then she lighted her lamp, set the bowls and the pewter in due order on the board, hung the samp-kettle over the rising blaze, and briskly forwarded preparations for supper.

Meanwhile, old man Joslin slouched into the big barn, and hearing Jotham's hacking cough in the hay-mow, mildly said: " You'd better go into the house, Jotham ; I expect your Ma wants you, for she's nigh out of firewood. I'll tend to the stock, and when Cal'line gits back from school (and it's nigh time), you tell her she needn't bother about the milkin'. I'll tend to that.''

Jotham, lean, long, and lank, slid down from the hay-mow, coughed his acquiescence in the plan laid out by his father, and went into the house, from whose keeping-room windows now streamed forth a ruddy light.

Elkanah watched the youth as he went across the dabbled snow. Then, leaning in the barn door, he gazed with dry and glassy eyes upward to the wintry sky, across which masses of cloud were driven. He marked the pale white moon, riding as if frighted, in the flying scud that hurried by. He looked with unconcern at the twinkling light of the sloop at anchor in the bay, and he thought to himself that she must have an icy berth over there under the lee of Orphan Island. Then, his face growing pale and ghastly as he turned from the dim and lonesome nightlight reflected from the snow, Elkanah felt his way along the familiar boarding of the barn, reached over and took from the cow-stall a halter that hung there, mounted to the hay-mow, threw himself upon his knees as if in silent prayer, climbed painfully and with many a half-uttered groan to the beam that crossed the barn from eaves to eaves, made fast one end of the rope around that timber, slipped the noose over his head, fitted it carefully around his neck, and, with firm-set lip, swung himself off into space.

The news that Elkanah Joslin had hanged himself in his barn travelled around the head of the bay in a leisurely manner. The discovery of Elkanah was not made by the family until some hours had passed. When Caroline came home from her distant school-teaching, she had taken the milking pails and had gone directly to the barn. Not seeing or hearing her father, she stood on the barn-floor, and cried " Oh, I say, Pa ! " but there was no response ; and it did not occur to the mind of this healthy and honest young woman that there was anything fearsome or weird in the utter stillness and darkness of the place. Only the grinding of the cows at their feed and the occasional grunt of the swine that were housed beneath the barn, disturbed the silence of the hour. So, tucking up her skirts, and singing a fragment of a camp-meeting hymn, like any modern farmer's girl, she went to work milking the three cows, one after the other.

Her mother, however, when Caroline returned with her brimming pails to the house, was more uneasy. Turning it over in her mind, she calculated that Pa had gone down the road a piece, to mend the fence where one of Robinson's cattle—Robinson's cattle were always straying up from their place—had broken through and had got at the fodder. She wondered what possessed him to go out on such an errand so late at night. He had had all day for that job. And she postponed taking up the supper, until Amzi, who was the youngest, and enjoyed his privileges as the spoiled child, made so great ado that she was fain to " dish up."

It was unusual for the head of the house to be absent from the evening meal. Jotham sighed as he looked at his father's empty chair. Caroline chatted about her day's experience in school. Amzi noisily absorbed mush-and-milk and fried mush deluged with New Orleans molasses, enjoying himself very much. The mother looked anxiously out of the window from where she sat, expecting to see the bent form of her husband trudge by on his way to the end door. But he never came. It was late in the night when Caroline went flying down the road to Captain Robinson's, with her white lips too tremulous to tell the doleful tidings to the frightened old man, who came and looked out at her as she pounded her small fists against the window-panes of his bedroom. He was speedily joined by Mrs. Robinson, also just awakened from her early sleep. Thence the news was carried up to Watson's by Will Robinson, the Captain's burly son. And Sally Watson, before she ran to comfort her bereaved friend Caroline, fled, trembling with cold and fear, still farther up the road to the Sellers's place, woke up the family, and besought Jim Sellers to go with her down to the Joslins. It was commonly reported in the neighborhood that Jim was keeping company with Sally Watson.

And so it came to pass that by two o'clock in the morning a small, but excited group of neighbors was assembled in the keeping-room of the Joslin place, each new recruit coming in with silent and cautious tread, as if afraid of waking the dead man, who lay in the best room on the other side of the front entry. The tea-things were taken up and put away by the first woman who came in. The family, in their terrified search for Elkanah, had let the supper-table stand untouched, after they rose to look for the missing man.

In those primitive days there was very little ceremony observed in the disposal of the dead. Before a week had passed, the snow was blowing dryly over the hillock of icy clods that marked the spot where the mortal part of the owner of

the farm had been laid, just outside of the till-
able land, where, with New England thrift, the
family burying-ground had been fenced off.
The suicide was a nine days' wonder in the settlement; yet Elkanah was not readily forgotten, for, after that night, the few incidents in
the uneventful history of the community were
dated from the time "when Elkanah Joslin
hung himself."

Ten years afterward, that is to say, in 1817,
after "the last war" was over, and peace had
returned to the distracted country, the sluggish
surface of life around the head of the Northern
Bay was once more stirred to its depths by the
story that sped from lip to lip. Jotham Joslin
had hanged himself from the identical beam
from which his father swung ten years before.
Yet it was not altogether surprising that Jotham,
hopeless of life, brooding over his father's tragic
end, and struggling hard to keep up his drooping spirits, should have finally succumbed to the
depressing influence of the big barn in which he
spent so much of his time. There was much
sympathetic comment on Jotham's provocations.
Some murmured that it was mighty queer that
two "professors" should have thus flown in the
face of Providence. For Jotham was a consist-
ent church-member, as his father had been.

Others said that the son was certain sure to go in the way his father went. "Sorter runs in the family," the aged Captain down the road remarked.

Very soon the people began to say that the Joslin barn was haunted. Not that anybody had ever seen or heard anything supernatural about that time-stained building. It was an honest-looking and commonplace barn. It even had two glass windows in it, which, in those times and in those parts, was an uncommon architectural vanity in a barn. But the neighborhood, with common consent, decided that it ought to be haunted, if any building ever should have been. And passers-by began to notice that the diamond-shaped opening in the gable next the road had a peculiarly wicked and sinister expression. "Looks like an evil eye," was what one of the Penobscot men said. And the remark was popularly approved.

It was in 1825 that Amzi Joslin, after having gone down to Ellsworth on a prolonged spree, returned home one hot August night, and without entering the house, softly let himself into the barn by the back entrance, and hanged himself from the now historic timber that crossed the edge of the hay-mow. Amzi had buried his mother and sister in the stony plot where his father and Jotham reposed under the gloomy and scanty turf. He was lonely, and his complaining wife and sickly baby did not enlighten the morbidness of his life. He had taken to drink, as many another poor fool does, hoping that in this he might drown his sorrows, none of which was very weighty or very unique.

"It's a sickly, pindling little critter," said the neighbors, of Amzi's only baby — Amzi junior. "'Twon't live to grow up. It's likely that it'll be the last of the Joslins in these parts."

But the infant Amzi lived to disappoint the croaking prophets by coming to manhood a hale, blithesome, and strapping young fellow. There was no trace of morbidness in the youthful Amzi's disposition. And when he married, and his buxom wife—an importation from Deer Isle—bore him a quiver-full of happy, hearty children, the old folks who had predicted the dying out of the Joslins slunk away to their appropriate burying-grounds, leaving the Joslins in contented possession of the homestead.

Nevertheless, the barn, with its tragic recollections clinging around it, stood, a perpetual reminder of the fateful ending of the career of three of the Joslins. Amzi often stood and looked at the fatal beam with a curious feeling of inquiry in his heart. If he had not been of a cheerful and sunny disposition, he would have dwelt with misgivings on the possibility of his, at last, coming to end his days on that timber. The thought sometimes flashed through his mind, but was quickly put away. Younger members of the family, to whom the gossips of the region had dutifully told the tale of the haunted barn, snatched a fearful joy in peering upward to the tragical beam in the darkness of the winter night, imagining that they saw a ghostly ancestor hanging there. But the young Joslins, as a rule, dreaded being in the barn alone after dark. Amzi never forgot what had happened there ; and he often thought, as he plodded about his work in the cow-bay, or in the mow, that it would be a mercy if the old barn should be struck by lightning and burnt to the ground. It was a sort of reminder, so he thought, to the children that might come after him. They would think of the three men who had taken violent hands against their own lives in that ancestral barn. He even asked himself if it were possible that, in his old age, with mental faculties dimmed and life a burden by reason of infirmities, he might not be enticed to his doom by the evil influences of the place.

But Amzi Joslin lived to a good old age,

and died as a Christian should, in his own bed,
surrounded by wife and children. All but one.
His oldest son, Rufus, went before his father.
The unhappy Rufus, inheriting a strain of the
" old Joslin blood," as the old women said,
followed after the ill example of Elkanah,
Jotham, and the first Amzi. No need for us to
tell how the good man wept over the sorrowful
tragedy of the young life snuffed out so need-
lessly, untimely. The old man aged swiftly
after this happened, and not a few of the community roundabout began to shake their heads
and whisper that old Amzi would go the way of
the other self-destroyers. But the farmer lived
on patiently and trustfully, dying, as we have
said, at a good old age and in a Christian
manner.

In 188–, after more than one generation of
Joslins had come and gone, the old barn had
acquired a name and repute throughout the
region altogether unenviable. It is not necessary nor desirable to tell here how two other
men of the Joslin family, as they grew up and
were old enough to take in the full significance
of the doleful story of the hereditary barn, became fixed in their belief that other suicides
must follow. Suffice to say that, in course of
years, but at long intervals, the historic timber

across the hay-mow bore evil fruit twice more. Something ailed the place, men said. There were strange lights about the farm o' nights. Sobs and whispering murmurs drifted down from the uplands on the wild March winds, or sighed in the snow-squalls that whirled around the place as the December gales came on apace.

No wonder that strangers, passing along the road, stopped and looked curiously at the barn, whose tragedy had been told at so many country firesides and in so many solitary wayside inns. It was the custom for every passenger along the road to turn his head and look at the old barn, now black with age, hoary with the gray lichens that clung to its roof, and still winking with its single evil eye in the gable. And when the Blue Hill stage drove that way, as it did when the upper road was heavy with the winter's snow, the passengers all craned their necks from the side of the wagon, and stared at the Joslin barn as long as it was in sight.

These things annoyed Mrs. Joslin, widow of Stephen, who had died in an honest and respectable manner. She knew that Stephen had worried a good deal over the *felo de se* of his father, and that he had had a fight within himself to keep back from the path which had brought so

many Joslins to the fatal beam. She knew that
her Stephen had sometimes thought that the
evil one was in that barn, and that he pursued
him—the oldest representative of the Joslin
name, continually suggesting that this was the
way out of the world for him. And so, although
her husband had never yielded to these wicked
thoughts, she had the family history so burned
into her very soul, that it fretted her to see the
gossiping people of the neighborhood whispering
and nodding their wise heads among themselves.
"If I was a Joslin, instead of a Gardner," she
would say, " I just believe that these everlasting
tattle-tales would drive me to hanging myself."

Not so thought Charlie, the widow's handsome and only son. Charlie was a prime favorite
through all the country-side. None so stalwart
and lithe as he. To see him swinging his scythe
as he strode down the mowing - field with
rhythmic step, levelling a mighty swathe, was as
good as a heroic poem on canvas. His melodious voice resounded like a trumpet when he
called to his oxen or chanted a rural ditty as he
came from a-field, hearty and fresh as if he had
not passed a long and toilsome day at the plough
or with the hay-rake. And many a country
lass, never quite unmindful of the tragic story of
the old barn, forgot it all when she looked into

Charlie Joslin's brown and handsome face. His dancing blue eyes, full of fun, and mild with the light of a cheery disposition, sent the tell-tale blush to many a coy young maiden's cheek, as she "passed the time o' day" with the young and thriving heir-apparent of the Joslin place.

But of all the girls that looked with a little thrill of rapture after Charlie's lithe and graceful figure, and marked the crisp brightness of his wavy hair, none seemed to have the power to arrest long his roving eye. It was a pity, too, the neighbors said, that Charlie should put off marrying. There was no knowing what might happen. The Joslins were a cur'ous family. There had been many mighty sing'lar things happening at the Joslin place. And Charlie was the last of the name. If he should live to be an old bachelor, he might get a twist into his mind, just as so many of the Joslins had afore him. Not that Charlie was the least bit tetched. He was as sound as a dollar. But there's no telling. And the wise ones shook their heads apprehensively.

If any of these croakings reached Charlie's ears, he gave them no heed. To him the blowing of the wind or the twittering of the swallows under the eaves of the old barn were just as worthy of a second thought as the idle gossip he heard among his mates, about the spell that so many thought rested on the Joslin farm. It was a wholesome place, he thought. The sun poured down its fulness, ripening the early harvest apples that hung in the dark green leaves of the little orchard, yellowing the grain that rose and fell in the upper field to the wanton-straying wind from the head of the bay, and giving the thick grass in the mowing-field a more intense emerald, day by day. It was a cheerful place, withal, in spite of the dark frown of the historic barn and the evil eye that twinkled in its gable. The hollyhocks and sunflowers drank in and yielded again, with a rapturous gladness of life, the warm sunshine and the languorous summer air. The very bees that kept up their murmurous song, as they filled themselves along the clover tops, and hied to the warm hives at the edge of the meadow, buzzed a cheery and satisfied hymn of peace and comfort. There was no room in Charlie's merry heart for foreboding of dark shadows of what might yet come. And if the thought of what had gone before ever crossed his mind, it was when, sinking into the tranquil slumbers of healthy and careless youth, he whispered to his innocent self that the jocund world was too good to leave.

Nevertheless, Master Charlie would not listen

to any suggestion that the barn should be torn
down.   There were timorous spirits in the vi-
cinity, who regarded the ancestral barn as a
blot on the landscape, a rallying point, perhaps, for the phantoms and hob-goblins of the
air and earth.   It is in the semi-farming and
seafaring life of a region like that around the
head of the Northern Bay that one must look
for a sturdy survival of all the old English pro-
vincial traditions and superstitions.   Here it is
that one is told of death-warnings, omens, signs
in the sky or on the waters, strange noises in the
woods, charms, love-potions, and occult devices
of various sorts.   No wonder that the ghost-
dreading folk who passed the Joslin place many
times in the year, looked at the barn in which so
many tragedies had been enacted, as something
quite too uncanny and unwholesome to be left
standing ; a standing invitation, so to speak, for
the last of the Joslins to come in and hang himself.   But the jovial master of the place would
not listen to reason.   He was not only sure that
he wouldn't take the fatal leap from the tradi-
tional beam, but that nobody else ever would.

"He just thinks the world-and-all of that
barn," grumbled one of the neighbors, surly
Major Payne, who, having come home from the
wars minus one leg and plus a pension, had set

himself up as oracle of the Northern Bay and Penobscot country.

" No, he wouldn't have a single board taken off that ere barn, 'cept it rotted off, for no money. I just think that Charlie Joslin considers that barn as a sort of ancestral tomb. So many of his relations have ended their days there, that's it's got to be a sort of sacred place to him. It may be sacred to him, but it's an infernal nuisance to the rest of the neighborhood. And that's a fact."

But there was one member of the Joslin family who really did wish that Charlie would tear down the fateful barn; and that was Nellie Webber. Now Nelly was only a hired girl in the Joslin place. Local usage forbids that we should call her a servant. She was emphatically one of the family, as all native-born family helps are in the region of which I am discoursing. The handmaid and the farm-hand are part and parcel of the household as long as they stay, sitting at the same board and respected as the children of the house, provided they are worthy of respect. They are, in fact, the children of other families, whose social standing in the widely scattered community is as high as that in which they temporarily serve; and of such was Nelly Webber.

Nelly's head was well filled with a goodly assortment of ghostly and supernatural lore. She could tell the stage of the tide by the cat's eyes; knew the best time for pig-killing by the phase of the moon; had heard drowned men's voices in the tide-rips hailing each other; was certain of the quality of the hay-crop when she had examined a bumble-bee's nest, and found significance in every incident of daily routine, from the dropping of a dish-clout to the color of the hen that had stolen her nest away.

And yet Nelly was not a sour and cross old maid, who took a savage pleasure in revenging on her fellow-beings the disappointments of her own life. Nelly was a merry and winsome fresh-faced country girl, from Blue Hill. She "lived out" because she did not like her step-mother, and because she had views in life that included the Normal School at Fairport, and the expenditure of more money than her second-wife-ridden father would allow her. Nevertheless, Nelly was strongly infected with superstitious notions, and she had a morbid aversion to the Joslin barn, and that aversion feebly extended to the Joslin family. But as her present engagement was the most eligible that had offered when she set out to "hoe her own row," as she was wont to express it, she waived the Joslin family ghosts, and accepted the situation with a lively sense of danger, which was not wholly without its charm to her adventurous spirit. And the cruel thing about this was, that Charlie loved Nelly. It was a long time before this awful yet pride-compelling fact dawned on Nelly's mind. For the shrewd girl was well aware that Widow Joslin had other views for her only son than a marriage with a portionless girl with a step-mother. Matilda Sellers, heir-presumptive to a farm on the other side of the river, and the ferry-right into the bargain, was a more eligible match for the handsome heir of all the Joslins.

It was in secret, and in fear of his mother's wrath, that Charlie carried on his wooing of the coy Nelly. Her birthday present from the young man was a " Friendship's Offering," gorgeously bound and gilt-edged, and bearing on its fly-leaf, in hastily pencilled secrecy, " Keep this dark." Sly Master Charlie meant to win the consent of Nelly, and then, secure in the possession of her love, brave the opposition of his mother. But the fair maid was obdurate. She vowed and protested that she was " keeping company with no feller ; " that she would " have nothing to do with beaux," and that until she had been through at least one term of the Normal School, when she should be fit to teach, she would have nothing to do with love or lovers.

"You're a hard-hearted and calculating thing," said Charlie, regarding her with new admiration, kindled by her very refusal to listen to his suit. "You'd be a regular tearer on a farm of our own. Gosh! how you'd make the help stand round!"

But compliments and hints were wasted on the matter-of-fact handmaid. She had laid out her career, and it did not include an early marriage with anybody, least of all with one of the haunted Joslins. So she shook her dancing curls at Master Charlie, and merrily defied him to come on with the allurements which he promised to add to those already set forth. The saucy beauty was a little pained, perhaps, to be obliged to say "no" to so handsome and likely a young fellow as Charlie. But Nelly had put her foot down, and when that remarkably well-shaped member was in an attitude of figurative determination, it was immovable. She loyally kept from the suspicious mother the secret that the young man had enjoined upon her; but she inwardly burned to let the gossips know that Charlie Joslin and the well-tilled farm could be hers for the taking.

Nellie's obstinacy only strengthened the determination of the wilful young man to win her heart. A more observant woman than Widow Joslin would have detected the courtship, vain as it was, that went on under her eyes. But she saw nothing. With a fierce repression, Charlie went about his round of homely tasks, laying out the work of the farm with a master's hand, and inspiring his helpers with his own cheery and lively temper, and enlivening the old place with his unfailing good-humor and blitheness. But the poor lad's heart was often heavy. Sometimes, when he caught a glimpse of the coldness that shone in Nelly's dark eyes, or was ravished anew by a sudden vision of her beauty, he made a half-choked excuse, and hurried away from the house, to forget his sorrows, if possible, in a long and impetuous walk over the wind-swept hills.

Many of the sharp-eyed women of the neighborhood noted Charlie's not unfrequent moodiness, fleeting though the clouds were on his sunny face. But they never suspected the cause of his disquiet. Even the loving vigilance of the mother failed to see that any serious grief moved the young man to behavior unusual; and nobody, not even the cause of all this perturbation, could know the anguish with which the rejected suitor, bent on gaining a revocation that seemed hopeless, buried himself in the hay of that fatal mow, and communed savagely with his fate. If Nelly could, at such times, have seen the exceeding great sorrow of her lover, mayhap she would have been moved to relenting. More likely, she would have been confirmed in her dread of the suicidal Joslins.

But there was no fear of Charlie. He contemplated his future with unclouded eyes, and his wholesome nature, hard though his lot might be, could not play tentatively on the verge of self-destruction. Nothing short of a blow that would be heavy enough to overturn his reason, could tempt the light-hearted Charlie to take a desperate step. And he yet had hope. He believed that Nelly was only trying him. She knew that he had a right to look higher for a wife. She would run no risks of dissatisfaction after marriage. She would not risk any possibility of having a difference in fortune " thrown up at her " when it should be too late to retrace her steps. And without taking so low a view of the case, Charlie revolved all these things in his heart, listening ever to the siren that sung of distant but possible bliss.

Master Charlie had a rude awaking. It was

in haying time, and the last load had that afternoon been hauled into the barn, and pitched to
lofts and mows. The day's work was done,
and silence and peace reigned over the Joslin
homestead, save where the heir of the farm
lightly leaned at the window and talked with
the girl who stood dawdling within the keeping-
room. The widow had gone down the road to
visit a sick neighbor. The tired farm-hands
had sought their unusually early rest. Only
Nelly and her persistent lover were left to
whisper together in the fast gathering darkness.
Great masses of black cloud were rolling up in
the westward, and a greenish crepuscular light
was filtered over the opposite shore of the
Northern Bay, suggesting a thunder-storm and a
summer rain.

No matter; the hay was all under cover, and
everything was made trim and snug for any
change that might come in the weather. But
this was not in Charlie's mind as he stood
there pleading by turns, and by turns bantering
the sorely beset young girl. He would not
take " no " for an answer, he said, and so he
foolishly rushed on to his fate.

" I should think you might give a man a decided answer," he said, half pettishly.

The girl's eyes flashed in the deepening

gloom as she tartly replied. "What do you want for an answer, Charlie Joslin?" she cried, with rising anger. "Haven't I told you fifty times that I wouldn't have you, nor any other man, for that matter? And what's more, I wouldn't marry a Joslin if he was to get down on his bended knees; and you know the reason why. So there, now!"

Master Charlie had got his answer. He went away half stunned, for the first time realizing in the cruel speech of the girl the depth that separated her from him. The flash of lightning that suddenly illumined the darkness in the western sky was not more vivid than the beam of light that had laid bare to the young man's mental vision the utter hopelessness of his lot. And, the face of nature changed to eyes that looked without seeing, he stumbled aimlessly and with sluggish step down through the orchard, whose fragrant fruit was brushed by his beautiful bare head as he passed beneath.

Big drops of rain were falling when Charlie, having mounted the highest upland swale on the farm, turned aimlessly and made his weary way back to the homestead. Reaching it he hesitated to go in, stood wondering which way he would turn next to be rid of the nightmare which pressed him down, and then wandered away again into the darkness like a lost man.

The Widow Joslin was scant of breath when she came hurrying home, scolding because the chamber-windows were not closed, although there was a smart shower coming over, and because Charlie had not come down the road after her, and she an old woman poking along in the dark. The rain fell in such sheets as it falls in a New England thunder-shower, or in the tropics, with a whirring and seething sound. The widow was always fidgety in a thunder-storm; her brother had been killed by lightning, and she never could abide thunder from that day to this. And she went complainingly to the rear of the house to make all fast, for the rain was pelting on the western windows.

" Land sakes alive ! " she screamed. " What a flash and crash ! I just believe that that struck somewheres nigh here. Did you ever, Nelly ? " and the frightened woman began to drag out a feather-bed, by way of shelter from the electric storm.

Just then, Nelly, whose face was turned away from the windows, saw a bright red light on the opposite wall of the room. She quickly turned her head, and, with a throbbing heart, cried, " Oh, Mis' Joslin, the barn's all afire ! "

The fatal hour for that ancestral edifice had come. It had been struck by lightning.

The Widow Joslin's fright vanished at the awful sight of the haunted barn in flames. With something like calmness, she looked, and only said, "I calculate that Charlie is out there fighting the fire."

The two women snatched such outer coverings as came to hand, and, while the widow went to the stair-door to waken the men with her shrill call, Nelly rushed out into the rain, crying "Fire!" with all her small might. It was needless. The bright flames flashed far and wide the signal of a great calamity. The neighbors ran breathlessly to the rescue, bearing the few buckets which formed the only appliance for extinguishing the fires that the region boasted. It was too late to save the haunted barn. Possibly, the men worked with less enthusiasm than they would have if the structure had been more highly valued in their eyes. They contented themselves with trying to save the house. The barn, with its stores of hay and grain, must go.

There was something awesome in the sight. A fire in the country is always more terrible than in the city. The flames are uncontrollable. The best that can be done, usually, is to confine the destruction to the building in which it has seated itself. But this fire raged on, while the rain fell hissing into the red ruin which it could not check. The thunderous artillery of the sky never ceased its booming volleys as the leaping fires sprang upward into the inky blackness of the night. And as the country-folk saw the charred framework of the old barn stand out with startling distinctness in the lurid light, they shivered to think of the tragedies that had taken place under the roof now flying from its place in red cinders, and had crept along that square stick of timber now blazing and crumbling before their eyes.

Were those fiery ghosts, or only shuddering flames, that went so swiftly off to the eastward, momently lighting up the gloom into which they vanished? Was that a cloud of burning hay that was swirled upward by the eddying draft of air? or was it some dreadful shape, some image of a dead and gone Joslin, hurrying away to a new rendezvous? and the fatal beam, would it never burn quite through and drop, an accursed thing? Nelly Webber wept as she looked ; wept, she knew not why. And her lively imagination saw dreadful things innumerable in the burning of the barn. And when the reddened skeleton fell in with a crash, and the volleying tumult of smoke and flame ascended on high, a suppressed shout that might have been a mighty sigh, and was very like a cheer, went up from the awe-stricken throng huddled on the rain-drenched slope before the house.

But where was the masterful Charlie while all this ruin was being wrought? The widow missed his voice cheering on the men. The men, even as they hurried about their arduous work, whispered ominously among themselves. And when the fire had died down, the other buildings saved, the horrible brightness quenched in an angry and sullen glare, and the widow had time to recover something of her scattered carefulness for other things than the ruined barn, she cried, with motherly anguish, " Where is that boy? "

And where was he? Returning, filled with rage and disappointment, to the group of build-ings of which the homestead was one, he had sullenly opened a side-door of the big black barn and looked in. Its great, darksome interior was filled with the fragrance of new-mown hay. The vivid flashes of lightning that illumined its mysterious depths showed rafter, mow, beam, and bay for an instant with startling distinctness, and then left the gloom deeper than before.

Twitterings of uneasy swallows nesting far up in the roof were the only sounds he heard, save when the thunder-peals rattled overhead.

"Curse the place!" It looked more cursed than ever as the young man muttered this malediction. He recalled Nelly's scornful answer to his last proposal; and now, as his eye wandered vaguely over the solid darkness within, he cursed the day that the barn had been built to stand a mute warning to all of the name of Joslin.

He stooped, drew a match across a plough-beam with a quick and nervous hand, threw the bit of lighted wood from him at random, darted out of the door, and fled breathlessly up the orchard-covered slope behind the house. Unminding the pelting of the storm, he sat long on the wet and mossy stone wall that divided the hill-top, watching the flames that lighted all the sky, touched the gables of the farm-houses far and near, and glittered on the fast-falling sheets of rain.

When, all the awkward efforts of the amateur firemen having failed to check the fire, the roof of the old barn fell in and a great fountain of flame spouted up into the heavens, Charlie recovered his spirits, and laughed loud and long. Standing up under the sky, now clearing after the rain, he cried : "Good-by, old barn ! No more Joslins will hang themselves from your rafters." Flame had purged the hereditary barn at last.

The fire was all over. The weary neighbors had been regaled in the farm-kitchen by the hospitable dame and had gone home, leaving two lonely women to their unwonted vigil ; for the mother would sit up until her boy's return, and the maid would fain bear her company. It was very strange, they thought, that the tumult of the fire, which had alarmed the country roundabout, from Fairport to Blue Hill, had not recalled the wanderer homeward. Neither of the women dared to confess the suspicion that haunted their thoughts. The horrible suggestion was unspoken, although each knew what was in the other's mind.

"You don't s'pose that Charlie went down to the barn to look after things when the storm came up ? " finally asked the widow as she set a candle in the window to guide the coming of her absent son.

"Deary me, no," replied the startled girl, her voice breaking as she spoke, and her heart contracting with a pang as when the dread possibility was forced upon her. Dame Joslin dropped, a forlorn and limp heap, crushed by a weight of woe, into the corner of the settle that stood by the chimney-piece. Nelly, for the first time giving voice to her fear, cried, "You don't think Charlie was in the barn, do you?" There was no answer, and the girl, on her knees by the settle, threw her arms around the sobbing mother, both wordless in their grief.

Thus they were huddled together in their loneliness as the storm went muttering off down the horizon and the stars came out. Nelly's quick young ear detected a stealthy tread on the door-stone. She raised her tear-stained face. The door swung open, and a shape stood limned against the misty night without. With a wild cry, "My darling Charlie!" the girl flew to him, flung herself against his broad bosom, and clutched at his beautiful head with a wild caress. In that supreme moment of joy she had confessed her love.

Needless to tell of the thankful mother's welcome, of her willing blessing on the twain, or of her sudden recognition of the tie that bound them all together. Any country-side gossip will tell you of these things if you journey along the Doshan shore and care to ask questions concerning the dwellers around the head of the bay. These are matters of local history now;

and the summer-boarder from Fairport, as he
saunters along the grassy lanes, or climbs the
breezy uplands overlooking the Narrows and
Orphan Island, will find berry-pickers and
herb-gatherers glad to narrate once more the
story of the haunted barn, and how it was struck
by lightning the year that the Helen Mar was
launched and Zeke Witham's cow fell down the
well.

The Phantom Sailor

THE PHANTOM SAILOR

I.

ONE sunny afternoon in October, just after the village school had been dismissed for the day, a sailor-like young fellow, apparently about twenty-five years old, sauntered down the main street of Fairport, Maine. The town, an old-fashioned seaport, now dead and dull, but in those far-off days tolerably active and bustling, is nestled on the side of a promontory which slopes to the bay on the east and to a series of coves and inlets on the west. The promontory is joined to the mainland by a narrow isthmus in the midst of a marsh, and the only highway from the town to the rest of the world passes over a narrow bridge built on the aforesaid neck of land, a canal having been cut across it by the British troops during the occupation of the place in the war of the Revolution. So, when the townsfolk beheld the stranger walking down their main street, they knew that, unless he had dropped from the skies, he must have come into the village over the neck and up the hill.

He was a handsome young fellow, with curly hair, and with a face tanned and roughened by the winds of many seas. He wore canvas trousers, once white, a checked shirt with a wide-rolling collar, and a blue jacket cut and trimmed in what is known as the "man-o'-war" style. On his head, jauntily cocked over his dark curls, was a flat knit cap without a visor, and of the pattern known as Scotch. He was in light walking trim, this seafaring stranger, carrying over his shoulder, lightly swinging from a stout stick, a bundle of "dunnage" tied in a bandanna handekrchief.

Into the back of his right hand had been pricked with a needle a female figure in red, presumably the Goddess of Liberty, leaning on a blue anchor. In the middle of his left hand was a cruel scar, that looked as if it might have been made by the thrust of a cutlass or a boarding-pike.

We boys had just been let out of school, and, whooping and racing down the common in very ecstasy of animal spirits, we were confronted by this somewhat unusual apparition. For, since the steam-frigate Missouri had made a call at the old port, several years before,

nothing like a man-o'-war's man had been seen
in town. The sailors of the fishing fleet, which
was then wont to flit in and out of the port,
were untidy and rough, and were clad, for the
most part, in odds and ends of garments which
were, as one might say, amphibious, since they
were worn in farming time as well as on their
short sea voyages. An occasional ship from Cadiz, or Liverpool, with a cargo of salt, brought
only a gang of sailors who never stayed in Fairport long enough to show any shore clothes, if
they had them. This alert young stranger, with
his rolling gait and seaman-like rig, instantly
arrested and fascinated our boyish attention.
We seemed to be brought face to face with the
romance of the seas. Here was a bronze-
cheeked man who brought with him from distant shores the odor of spices and the briny
wave. He had seen strange countries, perhaps
had fought pirates, nay, had possibly been cast
away on coral reefs or in the maelstroms of the
northern seas.

" Hullo, youngsters ! " he said, with a flour-
ish of his hand and an indescribable roll in his
voice, as if it, too, partook of the undulating
motion of the sea. So saying, he turned from
Main Street into elm-shaded and grassy Court
Street, followed at a distance by a small and

curious mob of boys. Village boys have a certain frank inquisitiveness which cannot be repressed by any conventional notions and which is very different from the curiosity of all other boys beneath the heavens, so far as my observation goes. A stranger in their village is like a new planet swimming into the ken of an astronomer. He must be watched, studied, and assigned his place in the phenomena of nature. So, when the seafarer turned the corner by the town-house, and walked down Howe's Lane, every boy within sight ran after him and watched him until he unhesitatingly entered the cottage of old Mother Hubbard.

Lest I do despite to the memory of an estimable old mother in Israel, now long since departed this life, let me say that Mrs. Hubbard was the widow of the captain of a fishing-smack, the John and Eliza, wrecked on the Banks, with all on board, in 1841, during the gale which is even now remembered with terror by the people of the New England coast. One of the Hubbard boys, Elkanah, was lost in the wreck of The Chariot of Fame, off the Bermudas, five years after, and the widowed woman, left with but one son, had vainly tried to keep the young man at home. But Lafayette

Hubbard ran away to sea in the bark Tonquin six years before the sailor of my tale walked down the village street ; and he had never been heard of from that day to this.

Mother Hubbard grew gray, wrinkled, and sad. She took in washing, went out among the neighbors in times of sickness and death, doing such chores as are most likely to fall to the needy and willing hands of a lone and childless widow. If she sometimes paused in the wringing of her clothes to wipe a salt tear that trickled down her nose, or if she turned her face hungrily toward the shining sea, while walking to and fro with some other woman's sick baby, it was because she was thinking of the absent and long-wandering boy. But beyond this, she made no sign of the mourning mother-love that slept within her aged breast. The neighbors, kindly belying their own convictions, would sometimes tell her that Lafayette might be alive and well in some far-off corner of the world, and that he would yet come home to make her old age happy. But there were too many places in the family circles of Fairport made vacant by wrecks that had never sent a token of the lost ones, for Mother Hubbard to cherish any hope. Her sorrow was common enough ; and so she said, as many another bereft one said, "I shall see him again when the sea gives up its dead."

In front of Mother Hubbard's door grew clumps of hollyhocks—red, white, and yellow. A few of these lingered yet on their tall stems, although the frosts had come. Standing afar off, we saw the sailor pluck one of the bright flowers, look into it with a smile, and cast it from him. Then he knocked on the door sharply with his brown knuckles, and, as soon as it was opened, he strode in and shut it behind him. Drawing nearer, we heard a crying and a sobbing within, mingled with the tones of a deep, manly voice. Mother Hubbard, as if she had heard the childish murmurs outside, came to the window and let down the green-slatted shade. But we saw that there were tears on her cheeks.

From lip to lip the rumor spread: Lafayette Hubbard had come home. He had brought a handkerchief full of gold, and gems, and precious things. He had been captured by a pirate, and had served on a slave-trader. He had also been on board of a man-o'-war, and had seen and heard all that belonged to a wandering sailor's life. It was as delightful as a story-book. Long time we boys hung around Mother Hubbard's cottage, waiting for the fascinating sailor to come forth and show himself. Some of the smaller boys grew tired of the long suspense, and went home to their bread-and-milk; for the short autumnal day was waning apace.

What went on in that weather-beaten little cottage none of us ever knew. But, as we whiled away the time with knuckle-down and mumble-the-peg, there grew a feeling that this might not be Lafayette Hubbard, after all. Perhaps he was only a wayfarer who had met him at sea and had come to bring tidings of the lost one. Perhaps—awful thought!—he had seen Lafayette die in a distant foreign land, and had mercifully come to relieve the poor mother of all uncertainty of her boy's fate. As these speculations grew, the door opened, and the young sailor settled all our doubts by saying, "I won't be gone long, mother." Then he kissed her withered cheek, and we knew that Lafayette Hubbard had come home at last.

The abashed boys slunk away from the stranger, who smiled cheerily and kindly at them as he lightly swung out of the little front yard, and so down Howe's Lane to Water Street. Good Mother Hubbard, with a shining face, looked after the sailor as he went down the steep lane, smiling and whispering to herself.

"Is that 'Fayette?" asked three or four boys at once.

"Yes, that's my boy," said the widow, with a little thrill of pride in her voice. "And I'm sure I'm dreadful thankful to the Lord that he has come home ag'in to his poor old mother. Thank the Lord for all His mercies! I give him up long ago. But it's him! It's him!"

Mother Hubbard did not commonly encourage the approach of the village boys. We all felt that she was happier when no boy was near her clothes-line laden with snowy linen. She seemed to think that a boy was a destructive and a soiler of all that was bright and clean. Bad boys stoned her hens, and other boys, not so bad, had sometimes trampled down her southernwood and camomile. But her joy now was great. She took us into her little cottage and showed to our wondering eyes a whale's tooth, elaborately carved and etched with designs of sea-monsters and mermaids. There was likewise a marvellous handkerchief, as it seemed to us, rainbow-tinted and sheeny in the sun.

"Almost too gay for his poor old mother's neck," said the widow, pensively, as she held it up to the light. "Then there is a bunch of coral, the rale red coral, boys, not the common white stuff," said the old woman. "Wal, now, I just wonder what has become of that coral," said she, musingly, looking around. "Wal, I guess Lafayette put it away somewheres."

And she mentioned the name of her long-lost boy with a certain unction which even we youngsters could not help noticing.

Sammy Hodgson, who always was a forward chap, asked the dame where Lafayette had been so many years. Mother Hubbard took a pinch of snuff, and said, as if addressing some far-off person :

"I s'pose six years seems like an etarnity to these younkers—but, dear me! dear me! it don't seem long to an old woman who has seen so many days and full of trouble." Then rallying herself, as it were, she explained. "Wal, you see, boys, Lafayette was took a prisoner on board one of them pirate ships that trade and plunder off the coast of Madagascar. He was sold into slavery somewheres onto the mainland; Afriky, I s'pose, and he didn't get a chance to get away until about a year ago, and ever since that he has been expectin' to come home to his poor old mother. Thanks be to the good Lord, he's come at last; and I'm too glad to ask any more questions, just now. He's goin' to overhaul his log, as he calls it, and reel me off the whole story, as soon's he gets rested."

This was delightful. We should hear "the whole story," too, some of these days. Meanwhile, the sailor who had been in the hands of the pirates, and had been sold into slavery on the coast of Africa, had gone down the lane, so his mother said, to see some of his old friends who lived on Water Street. He stayed at home only long enough to be sure that his mother was alive and well, and to assure her of his being the identical Lafayette Hubbard who had been gone away to sea for six years. There was the scar on his left hand, the scar of a cruel wound; how well she remembered it! and how well he remembered it! that scar made by a fish-hook fastened by some malicious boy in the backstay of the ship St. Leon, so that when 'Fayette slid down that way to escape the ship's keeper, he was caught by his hand.

"Dear suz me!" mused the old woman, "that seems only a day or two ago, and it's going on fourteen year!"

The sailor-man, turning to the left at the bottom of Howe's Lane, had walked along the street which skirted the bank overhanging the old wooden wharves of the port. Under the bank were cooper-shops, blacksmith-shops, and the like, and along its upper edge was a row of shabby cottages, the homes of fishermen, 'long-shoremen, and people who constituted the lower stratum of Fairport society. Into the house of the Drinkwaters the young sailor walked without so much as saying " by your leave."

The head of the Drinkwater family was the wife of old Bill Drinkwater, a dissolute and worthless elderly man, who lounged about in the sunshine, on the wharves, and under the fences, in the summer-time, and who often found his way into the poor-house in the winter. He was a ne'er-do-weel, but harmless, the butt of the mischievous boys of the port, and an object of contempt to everybody else, including even his wife, a shrill-voiced termagant, who was the terror of the neighborhood. The eldest boy of the family, Bill, was one of the absent lads of the town who had gone to sea and never had been heard of more. Bill, restive under the lashing of his mother's tongue, and ashamed of his father's vagabond habits, had shipped on board an English bark that had put into port, nine years before, with a cargo of salt. Beginning as a cabin-boy, when he had last been heard from he had worked his way up to be able seaman. But this had been four years before, and, in the meantime, news had come that he was on board the United States frigate Preble, which, as the reader may remember, was wrecked in the Bay of Biscay, in 1842.

Two of the boys who had attended the sailor to the door of Mother Hubbard's cottage had also followed him afar as he walked down the lane. Lafayette had gone to see the Drinkwaters. He had undoubtedly brought tidings of the missing William ! He had possibly seen him in foreign lands ! Perhaps Bill and 'Fayette had been in captivity together ! The thought was too enchanting to be seriously entertained.

While Nathan Dyer and Sylvanus Crawford stood and watched the shabby and dirty old house into which 'Fayette had disappeared, the door opened, and four or five of the numerous white-headed brood of Drinkwater children came tearing out and ran, a confused mob, toward the cooper-shop, where old Bill chanced to be employed for the day.

" Our Bill's got home ! '' shrieked the biggest of the train, Sal Drinkwater, a long-legged girl of nine years. She had heard of her absent brother Bill, but never until this day had she laid eyes on him. " Our Bill's got home ! " she cried to the neighborhood, as she sped down the bank, followed by five or six tow-headed infants of assorted sizes.

" Why, Vene, he's an impostor ! " said Nathan, looking at Sylvanus, with distended eyes. An impostor, I think, was really more novel and more captivating to the boyish imagination than a sailor who had been shipwrecked, taken by pirates, and sold into slavery. There was something horribly fascinating about an impostor. But why should we think that 'Fayette Hubbard, otherwise Bill Drinkwater, was an impostor ? Perhaps there was a mistake somewhere.

By the time that old Drinkwater, rather the worse for liquor, had unsteadily scrambled up the bank, attended by a band of gabbling infants, several of the boys who had been inspecting the premises of Mother Hubbard arrived on the scene and learned from Nathan and Sylvanus all that had been said and done. An excited company of lads accompanied old Drinkwater to his door. The aged vagabond was snuffling and sobbing.

" Yes," he said, " my pore Bill's come home to his pore old father. I hope's he's brought means with him so's t' keep his pore old father out of the pore-house, come winter.''

"'T'ain't Bill Drinkwater no more than I am,'' said Sammy Hodgson, stoutly. "It's 'Fayette Hubbard, if it's anybody. He's just been up to Mother Hubbard's, and she told us it was 'Fayette.''

"Hey! what's that, you young bunch of oakum?'' cried Bill Drinkwater, senior. "Not our Bill? Shet your head! I tell you, it's our Bill come home to his pore old father.'' And so, grumbling and wiping his eyes on the cuff of his tarry shirt-sleeve, old Bill stumbled into his own door. Marm Drinkwater, as she was generally called in the town, appeared on the threshold, and, with an angry face, assisted old Bill into the house, saying as she did so:

"Drunk ag'in! it's jist what Bill said he expected to see when he got to see you to home.''

The door was closed on the excited family group, and the boys, standing at a safe distance from the house, held a discussion as to what should be done. Some of the bolder ones were for going to Mr. Woods, the town constable, to lodge a complaint against "the impostor.'' Others thought the selectmen were the most proper persons to be waited upon. But Jo

Murch, making a speaking-trumpet of his hands, in the sailor fashion which was appropriate to the occasion, shouted at the house, "Impostor! Come out and show yourself!"

At this, the greater portion of the boys turned and ran a little way to await developments. Marm Drinkwater, scowling, came to the door. Shaking her fist at the panic-stricken huddle of boys, she cried:

"It's my Bill who has come home, ef you want to know. He's no impostor, I say. Ef any on you boys stay 'round here insultin' decent people, I'll break every bone in your bodies. Don't I know my own flesh and blood? Now, you jest clear out o' this!"

Greatly puzzled, and not without reasonable fears of Marm Drinkwater, the boys reluctantly sauntered off toward the village stores, which stood all in a row at the foot of Main Street. Others of the smaller lads went home, for it was nearly sundown, and the hour for supper was at hand.

While we were eagerly telling to those who would hear our strange tale of the sailor-man, Sal Drinkwater, the long-legged daughter of the family before mentioned, trotted along the dusty street with a yellow pitcher in her hand.

"Hullo!" cried Sammy Hodgson, "you've got an impostor down to your house!"

"I don't know what you mean by an impositor," said the girl. "It's our Bill. He's come home from Hijero, or some such place, and Pa has sent me over to Stearns's for a pint of rum. So, now! And there's the money that our Bill give me to pay for it." And the child, crossing the street, exhibited in the palm of her dirty hand, but with evident suspicion of the boys, a big silver dollar of Spanish coinage. "Now, then, I guess you're satisfied. Impositors don't sling 'round big silver dollars like that, do they?" And, so saying, Sal pranced away, proud of being the sister of a sailor who had come home from strange countries, after many years.

Mother Hubbard, getting out her slender stock of best china, and drawing from its retreat her only jar of preserved quinces—for 'Fayette had always had a sweet tooth—had made ready as inviting a supper for the returned prodigal as could be furnished forth from her stores. The pickles and the quinces were on the table, with the thin slivers of dried beef, and the brown loaf of Saturday's baking. Before the open fireplace was a tin of hot biscuits neatly covered with a towel, and the mingled

and delightful odors of Young Hyson tea and
toasted red herrings were diffused around.

The sun had set behind the fort, the revenue
cutter in the harbor had hauled down her flag,
and old Fitts, the barber, who never allowed a
lighted lamp inside his shop, was closing his
shutters. In Marm Drinkwater's house, a swarm
of hungry children hung around a table on
which unwonted luxuries were spread. The
Drinkwater children were always hungry, but
they had not been so expectant as now since
last Thanksgiving Day, when they had had a real
turkey for dinner. This was a festal occasion.
Bill had come home. There was cake on the
table, likewise white bread ; and ham and eggs
were frying on the stove. Bill had gone out to
see some of the neighbors, leaving behind him
a painted snuff-box of radiant colors, brought
from foreign parts for his mother, who was
always fond of snuff, as Bill well knew. And
he had not forgotten to fill the box with the
finest Maccaboy, a small bottle of which was
also included in his modest kit of gifts. For
Sal, born since he went to sea, he had brought
a handful of shells—love-shells, they were called,
delicate pink and white, with a golden tint
through the same.

And, while Mother Hubbard's supper waited

and the biscuits grew cold, and while Marm Drinkwater, having carefully covered the ham and eggs to keep them from the eager fingers of her young ones, gazed down the street and scolded to herself, Lafayette Hubbard, otherwise Bill Drinkwater, sat happily smiling in the poor and tidy room of Aunt Sukey Morey. We all called her Aunt Sukey, although she was neither aunt nor mother to anyone living in Fairport. Her "old man," as she used to call him, was lost at sea, years before, when her only child, Obadiah, was a baby. Obe Morey had grown up, and, not finding congenial work on the land, had gone to sea. He had come and gone on many a and prosperous voyage, until one dark and fatal year, when many a young life had been sucked down into the treacherous wave. It was while fishing on the Grand Banks, seven years before, that the Two Sisters was run down by a full-rigged ship, staggering along under double-reefed top-sails; for a gale was blowing, and the night was thick where the little "bankers" were riding on the fishing-grounds. Adam Bridges, the boy of the schooner's company, was picked up, sole survivor of the crew, and was brought into Thomaston by one of the fleet a few weeks afterward. Aunt Sukey heard the dread news with calm-

ness.   She was "used to sorrer," she said,
and, in the hearing of the town-folk, she made
no lamentation.   Her straw bonnet had been
decked with bits of black for many a long
year, and the only sign of her newer grief was a
narrow slab of gray marble in the burying-
ground, on which was cut a suitable inscription,
ending simply with " Lost at Sea."

And now, in the old Morey house, which
stood at the far end of the village street, the
last one in the straggling row, the young sailor
sat smiling, while Aunt Sukey stroked his
cheek, softly crying, under her breath, " My son,
my son, who was dead and is alive again ! "

In that strange and inexplicable way in
which news gets about a little village, it was
speedily known at the other end of the street
that Obe Morey had returned from sea.   At
least, a sailor who resembled Obe had been seen
going into the widow's home.   He had also
been seen chopping wood in the little shed
where Aunt Sukey stored her fuel, and when he
went into the house carrying an armful of stove-
wood, Mercy Mullett, unable longer to re-
strain her curiosity, made an errand into Aunt
Sukey's house.   While the old woman was
filling a tea-cup with the molasses, to borrow
which Mercy pretended to have come, the sly

young girl had kept her eyes about her. On the table was a bunch of bright red coral and a bandanna handkerchief, which, as Mercy Mullett well knew, had never before been in Aunt Sukey Morey's possession.

"This is my boy Obed, Mercy. You don't remember my boy Obed, do you? No? Well, I thought not. Land sakes alive! it's a long time since he was lost to me. Well, Mercy, this is Obed. The good Lord has sent him back to me." And the old woman beamed over the cup of molasses, which the girl nearly spilled on the floor as she stared at the handsome young sailor, who sat and smiled—only smiled—as amused by Mercy Mullett's confusion.

Alonzo Mullett, a contemporary of Obed Morey, hearing this report from his sister, refused to go into the cottage of the Morey family, now happily reunited. He straightway went over to Hatch's store and told all that he had heard. Four boys, lingering around the store, drank in with eager ears the tale narrated by Alonzo. It was not possible that this fascinating young sailor could be the long-lost son of three several women, although each had lost a son at sea, and each had acknowledged him as her own. It was too much for human belief.

It was also too much for the patience of four honest boys. Something must be done to unmask the impostor, for such it was now decided that the stranger must needs be. And so, as the sea-fog was creeping over the town, this volunteer police force proceeded to Aunt Sukey's. The light of a tallow-candle shed its little ray from the window of the house as the boys drew near. The sky beyond was gray with night and fog, and no sound was heard but the ceaseless murmur of the tide upon the beach.

A hurried council being held, four boys set up a shrill and incoherent yell. There was no reply. Then Sammy Hodgson, throwing into his piping voice as much manliness of tone as he could command, cried, "Bill Drinkwater! come out and show yourself!" There was something awesome and uncanny in this irreverent invocation of the name of one who had long since been numbered with the dead, and when the door was thrown open and the sailor rushed forth into the darkness and the fog, each individual boy took to his heels and ran as if for his life; nor did they stop until each was safe at home, where he told his tale.

Aunt Sukey had been bustling about her narrow room, making ready a late supper, for she had partaken of an early and frugal tea before her long-lost Obed had shown himself at her door. While she chatted with him, learning of his strange adventures on the Spanish Main, where he had been cast away twice, and where he had been severely ill with the Panama fever, she toasted a bit of salt codfish, pounded it soft with a mortar-pestle, buttered it, and put it by the fire; and, while she was carefully measuring off a drawing of tea, using the top of the tea-caddy for a measure, smiling to think that she need not be so economical now that Obed had come home, a shrill cry, as in derision of her joy, rose on the evening air without.

"Land sakes alive!" she cried. "What's them pesky boys up to now, I wonder?"

Then, as she wondered, she heard, with a chilly shiver creeping over her, Sam Hodgson's demand that Bill Drinkwater—Bill Drinkwater who had been drowned at sea—should come forth.

She put down the tea-caddy, dropping some of the precious grains of her Souchong as she did so, and looked at the young sailor. With something that sounded like an oath, he seized his cap and dashed out of the door; and he never was seen in Fairport from that day to this.

II.

ELEVEN years afterward, I had completed my education in school, academy, and college, and was at work, with all the kindling ambition of a tyro, on the great New England newspaper, which my readers will recall (at least the elder ones will), when I mention the name of *The Palladium.* It was my ambition, secretly confided only to my own heart and to Angelina, to be the editor-in-chief of *The Palladium.* But that consummation, so devoutly wished, was very far off, even to the most sanguine of young reporters " working on space " and paid at a very low rate indeed. But nothing is impossible to a young fellow who has his fortune to carve out for himself, and who has a strong imagination and vigorous health. Moreover, Angelina's father, who was employed in the custom-house, under a Whig administration, had promised us that we should be married when I should be promoted to a " regular sit," which meant that this desired event could only take place when I was on a weekly salary. So, of course, a great deal was possible; for a great deal was to be done.

The crisis came for me most unexpectedly one wild and stormy March evening. I had planned to help Charley Whiting on the musical and dramatic that night, for that would give me a chance to take Angelina to see Warren, and I had promised to call for her if Charley would only agree to my proposition.

At half-past six, just as Charley came panting up the stairs that led to the editorial rooms, old Sanger came out of his den with a bit of ship news in his hand. Sanger was usually known as "Old Salt," for he was the shipping-news editor, and knew, or thought he knew, more about ships, shipping, and navigation than any other living man. Seating himself carelessly on one corner of the musical and dramatic desk (and only Old Salt and the editor-in-chief were allowed this familiarity), Mr. Sanger asked:

"Does anybody in the city-room know anything about the reported fall of the Sargent's Ledge light-house?"

Of course, nobody knew anything of the kind. If he had, it would have been his duty to tell of it as soon as he could run to the office. For *The Palladium* prided itself on being ahead of every other newspaper in the United States, not to say the world. Jerry Collins did say, however, that there was a rumor down among the wharves and docks that Sargent's Ledge light had gone down in the March gale that had prevailed for three days past. But Jerry, who was a born newspaper man, and who, poor fellow! was killed at Port Hudson years afterward, while in General Banks's command, had not been content to abandon this as a rumor until he had run the thing down to what seemed to have been merely the statement of an ancient mariner that "if this here gale continnered, Sargent's Ledge light would hev to go."

Then Old Salt read, with great deliberation, from his slip as follows: "Herm. brig William & Sally, from Fairport, Maine, with a cargo of codfish to Hemmenway and Sons, February 27, reports heavy weather outside; shipped a sea in N. W. Channel, and lost one able seaman, Timothy Holbrook, overboard; also deck-load of lumber. The light on Sargent's Ledge was not burning. Snow flying thick at the time, and heavy sea running."

"The skipper of the William & Sally may have been deceived," said Mr. Sanger, shaving his cheek with the edge of his right hand, as was his wont, while he scrutinized the bit of paper before him. "He may have been deceived, for the snow was blinding, and it must have been dusk when he passed Sargent's Ledge, off Sequansett."

The old man, solemn with importance, passed into the Chief's room, from which there presently came a summons for Jerry Collins to appear. There was a long and anxious consultation, at the end of which the Chief came forth, followed by Old Salt and Jerry.

"There is a reasonable ground for believing that Sargent's Ledge light-house has been swept away by the gale," said the editor-in-chief, "and it is very important that *The Palladium* should have the facts. I have decided to send one of you young gentlemen to Sequansett to ascertain the facts. Mr. Guild, what time does the next train for Sequansett leave the Old Colony depot?"

Mr. Guild consulted the time-table and said :
"Half-past six, sir."

"Half-past six!" said the Chief, with a faint show of excitement. "Half-past six! Why, zounds, sir, it is now twenty-seven minutes past!"

Guild bowed his head meekly, as if he were responsible for the lateness of the hour, and murmured :
"True, sir."

"And this is the last train to-night, I take it, Mr. Guild?"

"No other train out until eight-twenty to-morrow morning, sir," answered Guild, sadly.

A solemn stillness prevailed in the office, and we could hear the ticking of the old clock in the tower far above our heads. It was, indeed, a crisis. In those days there were no telegraphic wires ramifying through every part of the country. One line connected two or three of the largest cities on the Atlantic seaboard, and over this we received, every night while Congress was in session, at least two hundred words, giving the fullest summary of all the important news from the national capital. There were very few railroads, and many queer devices, unknown in these modern days, were resorted to by the news-gatherers. Our European advices were sent from Cape Race by carrier-pigeons, and the arrival of an ocean steamer mail, with a new part of one of Charles Dickens's stories, was an event to be celebrated by the issue of an extra edition of *The Palladium.*

But here was a bare possibility that Sargent's Ledge light-house had been destroyed, and *The Palladium* would be obliged to come out in the morning with nothing more than a paragraph beginning with that hateful phrase, "It is rumored." It was not to be thought of. Sargent's Ledge light-house was one of the wonders of modern engineering and architecture. It was built on a set of iron stilts, so to speak, the iron bars being sunk deep into a ledge of rock, and the light-house perched at the apex of the structure, like a martin-box at the top of a pole. There must be a light on Sargent's Ledge, and the contriver of this structure had offered to show his faith in its power to endure the storms of the Atlantic by taking up his permanent residence in the house. But there were reasons why this handsome offer could not be accepted. And now to think that the famous light-house should be swept away and *The Palladium* not be able to say anything about it next morning! The thought was madness.

"We'll have a special engine!" cried the Chief.

It was as if we had had an electric shock. Every man started, and each was only restrained by the severe discipline of the office from crying "hurrah!" In those far-off days, newspapers did not run special trains or have special despatches, and the determination of our illustrious Chief to hire a special locomotive to go to Sequansett for the verification of a rumor was Napoleonic.

"What is the run to Sequansett, Mr. Guild?" asked the Chief.

"An hour and forty minutes, sir," said Guild.

"An hour and forty minutes will give us time to spend two hours in Sequansett gathering the news, if there is any (and let us hope there is none)," said the Chief, reverently, "and time to get back to the office at one o'clock in the morning. Mr. Gay, you may keep back the forms until two-fifteen—not one minute later. We shall be back in time to have the facts, whatever they may be, in every edition of the paper."

This was decisive and to the point. But the Chief had not intimated who was to go on the expedition of high emprise. I thought of Angelina and of Angelina's father's promise, and perhaps I showed in my expression my eagerness to go. Looking around the office, with a queer air of searching for somebody, the Chief said :

"We will give this task to the youngest man on the paper. Mr. Rivers, take your instructions from Mr. Gay. Go to the publication office for money to pay your incidental expenses. I shall send Mr. Oliver at once to the station to engage the locomotive to carry you on your journey, and I wish you great success and as pleasant a trip as can be expected under the circumstances." So saying, the Chief turned and re-entered his private office.

To say I was delighted at my unexpected good luck, even transported, would faintly describe my elation. My associates crowded around me with hurried congratulations, wishing me success, and expressing their envy of my great good fortune. I felt like a young Columbus, fitted out with a fleet and gifted with all the means for a voyage of discovery.

"What if there is nothing in the rumor?" Of course it was Guild who threw this damper on my spirits. Guild was always saying unpleasant things.

"Then *The Palladium* will be the only paper to say to-morrow morning that there is no truth in the rumor that Sargent's Ledge light has been destroyed," said Old Salt, proudly.

"Good for you, Old Salt!" cried Jerry Collins. "Spoken like a true newspaper man. We will have a display head, whatever happens. It will be a big sensation, anyhow; and the old *Palladium* as usual, will lay over all the other papers."

But there was no time for idle talk. I must be away from the station by seven o'clock, at the very farthest, and every minute now was precious. I had no time to go to see Angelina, but I scribbled a line to her on the back of a visiting-card as I rumbled and rolled in an omnibus that took me within a half-square of my lodgings. I informed Angelina that I had been sent out of town on a most important errand, and that we must give up seeing Warren, for that night, at least. My landlady's son, a freckled-faced urchin of tender years, was glad to run with this message, stimulated by a promise of handsome reward. With joy and excitement I hurried on a few extra wraps, for the night was bitter cold, and I was soon rushing out of the Old Colony depot on a locomotive bound for Sequansett.

There is no need to tell of the flying and exciting trip to the south shore. The engine rocked from side to side, unbalanced as she was by any weight of train. The snow flew over the roof of the little cab in which we were ensconced, the engineer and the fireman taking turns at keeping a lookout ahead. But there was no danger of a collision; we had the road to ourselves until next morning at eight-twenty. There was no telegraph wire, however, to warn of our coming, and it was within the bounds of possibility that some other special engine might be out in the thick, dark night on a mysterious errand. Breathless we sped along, plunging into the darkness, shooting through quiet and sleeping villages, or anon rushing past a red light in the storm which showed where tavern-tipplers were lingering over their hot toddy, loath to go home.

I dozed in a corner of the cab, even the excitement of the trip failing to keep me awake, for I had been up late the night before, and the monotony of the rattle of the locomotive lulled me to sleep. The hour and forty minutes stretched to two hours before the engineer, shaking me by the shoulder, cried, "Look sharp, young feller, we're coming into Sequansett medders."

Sure enough. I recognized the long stretch of salt meadows, now dimly seen through the driving snow, which skirt the ancient town of Sequansett. The engine was slowed up as we rumbled over the bridge that spans Smith's Run, when the fireman, turning his gaze seaward for an instant, cried, "By Jehoshaphat! the light's gone out on Sargent's Ledge!"

The village of Sequansett was as quiet as the grave when we rattled into the engine-yard near the station, to the great amazement of the only watchman on duty. To this man, rough and amphibious in appearance, I at once addressed myself.

"Tell me," I said with an anxious feeling that my errand might, after all, be bootless, "how about Sargent's Ledge light? Has anything happened to it?"

"Happened to it?" said the cynical half-salt, half-farmer, "Wal, yes, she's gone to pieces, slick and clean; nothin' left but a passel of crooked braces. But you can't see 'em— too thick to see anything."

Then it was true! My journey had not been undertaken for nothing. *The Palladium* would have the only account of the loss of Sargent's Ledge light, to-morrow morning. But how to get that account! The Amphibious could not tell me anything about it. He only knew that the light-house was gone, and that the people in the village could not have seen it go, even if they had been watching for the catastrophe. The weather had been thick for two days. "As thick as all possessed," the Amphibious said. It had been reported, however, that Dan More, "a lobsterer," who lived at the edge of the shore, "just beyond the ma'sh," knew something of the affair.

It was said that he had seen the light-house fall.

"Was not anybody saved from the people in the light?"

"Nary one. Seven on 'em. Not one ever heerd on since the storm set in. Pore critters! They all went together."

From the Amphibious I learned the way to Dan More's hut, a lonely habitation where lived a recluse, in ill repute with the villagers, who seemed to resent his solitariness as something like a personal slight upon the whole body politic. He was "sort of shaky in his upper story," the Amphibious said, plainly meaning that he was different from all the rest of the villagers in his non-communicativeness. Here was an unpromising subject for an enterprising reporter. But the difficulty of the situation only inspired me with new zeal as, leaving directions with the engineer as to our future movements, I pushed my way across a dreary waste of snow.

After a long struggle with the blasts that blew across the shore and marsh, and with the uneven and half-obliterated road to the beach, breathless and tired, I reached the door of a cabin, one half of which had been adapted from a ship's caboose and the rest from the spoil of farmer's fences, and all of which was as black and forbidding as a witch's hovel. A vigorous knock on the door of the hut brought no response. A few kicks and thumps were no more successful. All was darkness and silence. Perhaps the old man was not at home. And he was the only person who could give *The Palladium* the account that must be printed to-morrow morning !

I tried the latch of the door. It was fast, but the rattle of this primitive contrivance evidently aroused the solitary inmate, for he called out :

" Hullo, there ! "

" Does Mr. Daniel More live here ? " was my answer.

" No, but old Dan More lives here," was the surly reply, and I heard the creaking of boards, as though somebody was getting out of bed and shuffling over the floor. Then there was an unbarring of the door, and, by the reflected light from the snow, I caught a glimpse of a shaggy figure half-clad and evidently just aroused from sleep.

" I have come down from the city, Mr. More," I said, " to get the particulars of the destruction of the Sargent's Ledge light. I understand that you saw it ? "

"Yes, I seen it go, and an everlastin' shame it was; but how did you come from the city at this time o' night? The last train got in more'n half an hour ago. Don't b'lieve you." And the man looked at me with an unpleasant expression of suspicion, perceptible more in his tone of voice than on his face, for it was too dark to see that.

"I came down on a special engine," I explained. "I belong to *The Palladium*, and we want to print an account of the disaster in the paper to-morrow morning."

"Wal, I swan to man!" said Daniel More. "Come in."

Once inside, and in the presence of the man who had seen the light-house go to wreck, I felt my spirits rise. More struck a light, and, as the feeble rays of the candle illumined his face, I saw a handsome though sea-beaten visage, black curls plentifully mingled with gray, and a full gray beard that swept his naked and hairy breast. There was something familiar in his manner, as if he were someone whom I had met in a previous and far-off state of existence.

Holding the candle close to my face, as if to scan every lineament of it, he looked me carefully all over, from the fur cap on my head to

the snow-covered boots on my feet, and said
again, " Wal, I swan to man ! "

Then, placing the light on a table made from
a flour-barrel, he stirred open the fire from the
ashes and embers, threw on an armful of drift-
wood, and said :

" Wal, youngster, begin."

" But I want you to begin," I said, with
some impatience, for the precious time was fast
slipping away, and this ponderous old fellow
showed no sign of being ready to communicate
anything.   " Now then, lie down in your bunk
there, and tell me what you know about the destruction of the light-house ; that's a good fellow ; when did it happen ? "

Daniel More deliberately tumbled into his
bunk, looking curiously at me, and making once
more his remark of astonishment.   Then, slowly settling himself for a chat, he asked :

" Be you one of them reporters—one of them
fellers that write for the papers ? "

I told him that I was, and that I should be
very much obliged if he would tell me his story
as soon as possible, as I must get back to the city
by one o'clock at the very latest.   With that I
whipped out my note-book and pencil, seated
myself on a box near the side of the bunk, and
waited for Dan to begin.

"It was a wild and stormy day nigh the end of March when an oncommon gale from the nor-nor-east——" he began.

"Hold on! hold on!" I cried, in dismay. "That's not the way. Tell me just what you saw, in your own language. I'll put in the big words afterward."

"What, young man!" said Dan, raising himself on his elbow and looking incredulously at me. "Do you mean to say that my story isn't a-goin' into the paper?"

"Certainly it is, but not in that way. Can't you understand? I shall put in your story and not your talk."

With some difficulty I impressed on the puzzled man the idea that he was to tell me all he knew in as simple language as possible. Then he settled himself, and went on with his tale.

It is not necessary that I should retell the old and tragical story of the wreck of Sargent's Ledge light-house. Daniel More was the only witness who beheld from the shore the fearful disaster wrought by that wild March storm. His tale has become, in the lapse of years, a sea-side classic. And I am proud to say that the narration first found publication in the columns of *The Palladium.*

But Dan had been out all day, and during

the night before, doing what he could to find
the bodies of the lost and wrecked from the
light-house. I did my best to write down his
exact words, but he repeated himself so often,
and so doubled on himself, and used so many
localisms, that it was difficult for me to keep the
run of his talk. Every now and then, after trying to straighten out what I had written, I would
raise my eyes from the fish-box which served as
a writing-table and cry, " Now go on, Mr.
More ! " only to find him fast asleep. The night
was wearing away, and I would fly at him, shake
him vigorously. Then he would cry, " Avast
heavin' ! " and begin again with a sleepy igno-
rance of all that had gone before.

Once, with the perspiration oozing from my
forehead, as I began to fear that I might fail,
after all, I was aroused by a tremendous snore.
I looked at the mariner with something like anguish. Here was this unfeeling wretch fast
asleep, and everything depended upon his story
being printed in *The Palladium* next morning.
I thought of Angelina, of Angelina's father in
the custom-house, of the fellows in the office
who would envy or deride me, according to my
success or my defeat, and of the Chief, who
could make or unmake me. And there was that
aged ruffian fast asleep.

In his sleep he looked more than ever like the handsome young fellow whom I must have met in some previous state of existence. As I shook him again, my eye fell upon his right hand, on the back of which was tattooed the device of a red lady leaning on a blue anchor. Like a flash, it all came back to me. For an instant I forgot the light-house on Sargent's Ledge, *The Palladium*, and even Angelina and Angelina's father. I saw a bronze-cheeked and handsome young sailor sauntering down the green lanes of Fairport, swinging his bundle and stick as he walked into Mother Hubbard's door-way.

Turning heavily, the old impostor muttered, " It's all along o' them blasted cables that the lubbers rigged out for braces. If it hadn't been for them, Sargent's Ledge light——" The rest of the sentence was lost in an inarticulate gurgle.

Shaking him once more, I bawled into his ear :

" Halloo, there ! how are you, 'Fayette Hubbard ? "

Mr. Daniel More struggled feebly into wakefulness, and said, peevishly :

" Le' me alone ! I thought you had got through."

And he was sinking off to sleep again when I cried :

" How are you, Bill Drinkwater ? How are you, Obe Morey ? "

The aged sinner sat up, wide awake.

" Oho ! " he laughed with glee. " I guess you're a Fairport boy."

I acknowledged that I was, and, although the pressure of my errand came back upon me with redoubled force, and the time was fast flying, I could not help asking him why he had been tempted to personate three missing men, and thus to cheat three poor women into the renewal of an old grief.

" Wal, you see, youngster," he explained, " I was a-voyagin' with all three on 'em. They was smart boys. I met 'em, one after another, in them wild days of mine. We was chums, we was. That is to say, we was messmates, at odd times, and friends allus. When I heerd tell that 'Fayette Hubbard was lost on the coast of Afriky, I felt mighty bad. And, three year afterward, when I was told that Bill Drinkwater and Obe Morey, all from the same place, had gone to Davy Jones's locker, it seemed kind o' like a special providence. Yes, it did."

" And so you thought it would help things

along if you went to Fairport and lied to the poor old women?"

"Avast heavin' there, young feller! I didn't do no such a thing. I was in Belfast, discharged sick, and was to be sent to the Chelsea Hospital. But I was took in hand by a clever old lady. She kep' a sailor boardin'-house, and set me on my pins ag'in. Just then the Old Nick happened to put it into my head that I might take a run over to Fairport and see the old folks. I had never be'n there, and I thought I would go over and see what it was like. The Fairport boys as you hev mentioned was allus a-braggin' about the place. So I made a bargain with a lumberman to set me ashore as he went up the Penobscot to Bangor. I had be'n to Bangor before."

"And you walked down and across the Neck to Fairport?"

"Exactly. I walked down to Fairport, and on my way I thought it might be a good joke to see if I couldn't pass myself off as one of them missin' boys. But Lord! young feller," and here the old scamp cackled loud and long, "I didn't think to play this off on the very mothers that bore 'em. But I did, though— blow me if I didn't!"

There was no longer any need to shake Mr.

Daniel More in order to keep him awake.
Even his surliness melted away. He sat up in
his bunk, told me his tale as connectedly and
lucidly as he could, and, while I labored with
my pencil, he diverted himself, in the intervals,
with looking at me and grinning silently. Once
or twice he roared with laughter, and then,
checking himself, cried:

"But I fooled 'em, all three—blow me if I
didn't!"

Perhaps he felt a pang of remorse, too, for he
once put on a serious look, and said:

"Wal, youngster, if it's any favor to you,—
a Fairport boy, like my mates as was,—I'll give
you the best I've got by way of story. But,
Lord! young feller, I can't spin a yarn like I
used to could! But I did fool them old ladies
—all three on 'em."

Daniel went on with his story, bit by bit,
and I had it all in hand. I knew that Jerry
Collins was hard at work in the office over-
hauling the files of *The Palladium* and getting into shape all of the collateral branches
of the subject in anticipation of whatever I
might bring back from Sequansett. I could
give the finishing touches to my manuscript
as we bowled along in the engine, homeward
bound.

I gathered up my notes with feverish haste. Daniel assisted me with my wraps, with rough officiousness. Stroking down my coat-skirts with a bear-like familiarity, he said:

"Wal, I'm dretful glad to hev seen ye, young feller, and, if you ever come this way ag'in, jest drop in and see a feller."

I shook him heartily by the hand, assured him that I would send him two copies of *The Palladium* next morning, and would come again and see him, some day, and get all of his marvellous tale of the sea.

I had solved two mysteries, and I felt myself repaid for years of waiting and for much anxiety and labor. With something of the thrill of a conqueror I ran across the howling waste of snow and marsh, and Daniel More, with his hands at his mouth, speaking-trumpet-fashion, bawled after me: "I say, shipmet, give my love to my three mothers when you go to Fairport ag'in." The convicted impostor had no pangs of contrition, after all.

My return to *The Palladium* office, burdened with the tale of the destruction of Sargent's Ledge light-house, was like a triumph. I was in time for the morning edition, and Old Salt received me with genuine enthusiasm.

Even Guild relaxed a little from his stately professional dignity, and Jerry fairly danced with joy. The Chief had gone home, leaving minute directions as to the use to be made of my news, whatever it might be. When all was done, and the paper had gone to press, with extra precautions taken against the purloining of our news from an early copy of *The Palladium* by some wicked rival, I sought my lodgings, and, proud and happy, sunk into the sleep of the just, my last thought being of the elation with which the Chief would read next morning, in the old *Palladium*, the exclusive account of the destruction of Sargent's Ledge light-house. It all came true. We had the news to ourselves, and took the town by storm.

When I think of those unhappy creatures who perished in the wreck of the light-house, and remember that their fate was so closely linked with mine, I cannot suppress a feeling of sadness. Perhaps I might have gained my promotion and Angelina in some other way. But all that is conjectural. It always seemed to me that if the fall of the light-house had not come just as it did, and if I had not been sent just as I was, and I had not found that impostor of the sea just as I did, every-

thing in life would have been very different
with me.

And that is the reason why I proposed to
Angelina, a year or two afterward, that Sargent's Ledge should be perpetuated in the
family. But Angelina said, with a great show
of merriment, that Sargent's Ledge was not a
proper name for a child. She had her own
way, of course; but, somehow, the youngster
is always known about the house as the Phan-
tom Sailor; and this is the reason, I suppose,
why he declares that he will go to sea as soon
as he is big enough.

The Honor of a Family

THE HONOR OF A FAMILY

I

"THREE lights a-burnin', and nary ship at sea!" So saying, the mistress of the poor-house blew out one of three candles, all in a row.

Three old women looked up from their sewing, and the least aged said:

"Land sakes alive, Mis' Rogers! don't the taown find us in candles? What's the use of bein' so pesky stingy abaout light?"

"The town finds you poor folks in candles, but not to waste," said the matron, with severity. "And 'wilful waste makes woful want' —which is the reason why some folks is in the poor-house instead of bein' to home and under their own ruff."

This pointed rebuke silenced the old woman, who resumed her sewing, which was on a long white garment, ghastly and cold. One of the old women who was sewing on the other end of the work spoke up and said:

" This shroud is e'enamost done, and I cal'-
late it'll be wanted to - night. I looked at
Emmy a little while ago, and she seems to be
failin' fast. Don't you think so, Mis' Rogers?"

The poor-house mistress, with a shade of impatience in her voice, replied :

" Wal, I s'pose so. It's low tide at two in the
mornin', and I rather guess she'll go out on the
ebb tide. They mostly do. Goodness knows
she's been long enough a-gittin' ready. The
town of Fairport had no call to throw her onto
us ; and if I had been one of the selectmen of
Murchville I'd have kerried it into the county
court afore I'd have stood it."

The idea of Mistress Rogers carrying an appeal into the court seemed to awe the three old
women ; and one of them, dropping her voice
to a low whisper, and looking toward a half-
open door, through which could be seen a
dimly lighted sleeping-room, said :

" Can't you get her to tell the name of the
father of that child of her'n before she goes?
She's dretful particular, seems to me, to carry
that secret into the grave with her."

" 'Tain't no use—not the least bit. I've
coaxed and coaxed," rejoined the mistress,
" but it don't do the least mite of good. I
should admire to know who was the father of

that child; but she holds onto it like grim death, and she'll kerry his name, whatever it is, down in sorrer to the grave with her."

A low moan from the next room attracted the attention of the mistress, and, removing the candle which she had just extinguished, she betook herself to the side of poor Emmeline Kench, who lay a-dying in the Murchville poor-house.

There had been a long dispute betwixt the towns of Fairport and Murchville as to which of the two should be held responsible for the support of Emmeline Kench, a pauper. There was a time when the woman who now lay waiting for death was a bright, winsome, and giddy girl. Hers was that delicate and fragile beauty which, among the inhabitants of the Maine sea-coast, too often betokens a tendency toward consumption. She was the daughter of 'Siah Kench, an old vagabond, who maintained himself by doing odd jobs about the wharves of the "Port," as the village of Fairport, on the other side of the harbor, was called. 'Siah had been left a widower when his wife gave birth to Emmeline, and the child grew up in the houses of those of the charitable who were willing to receive her, after she had been duly nursed into girlhood at the poor-farm of Fairport. As soon as she was old enough Emmeline went out to service, and adopted the calling of "hired gal" as her own.

People wondered whence the girl got her remarkable beauty; she seemed as frail and fair as a lily. Her delicately moulded face was tinged with the color of a cinnamon-rose; and her golden hair, usually flying in the wind, to the great scandal of the staid townsfolk, was of that silken fineness which poets rave of and seldom see. Nobody remembered her mother's looks. She had left behind her only a vague memory of a faded, unkempt, ill-clad woman. But there was her father, slouching about the wharves every day—a hard-featured, frowsy fellow, with a battered sou'wester on his head, and wearing garments that had been so often patched and darned by his own weather-beaten hands that no man could tell what was their original color or material. Old 'Siah did not look as if his was the parent stock from which this delicate flower had sprung.

But, notwithstanding her apparent fragility, Emmeline was by no means a feeble creature. Wherever she went among the families of Fairport and Murchville—and she changed her place full often—she made herself welcome as "a masterhand to work." She could milk,

make butter, and do the general housework of a
large family; get out a big week's washing
before most other girls were astir in the morning; and could, on a pinch, sally forth to the
wood-pile and chop her own fuel. Once, when
some of the curious neighbors who lived on the
Fairport common heard somebody loading a
wheelbarrow with chips, night after night, at
the new school-house, and go whistling down
the path, they discovered that it was Emmy, who
took this method of providing her kindlings.
And once, when Bob Booden, a rough fisherman of the Port, attempted to kiss the wilful
girl, at an apple-pearing-bee, she cuffed his
ears so soundly that the water stood in his eyes
as he groaned, "Gosh! the gal's got a fist like
a man-o'-warsman."

Fickle, unstable, and hard to please, Emily
flitted from family to family, but oftenest hired
her services to the Grindles, a staid household
of Murchville. This village is an old-fashioned one, opposite Fairport, inhabited by a
few scattered dwellers by the sea-shore, who
earn a livelihood by tilling the ungrateful
ground, fishing in the bay, and chopping, with
sparing hands, the scanty growths which cover
the hills back of the village. The Grindle
family were said to be "forehanded." It was

commonly reported that they had money out at interest; and it was a matter of public concern that they owned a sixteenth of the ship St. Leon, trading to foreign parts, and returning once a year to Fairport with a cargo of Cadiz salt.

The Grindles lived in one household, after the good old patriarchal fashion, in a big, gambrel-roofed house, on a bluff that over-looked the harbor and the village of Fairport on the further side. "Old man Grindle," as he was called by his neighbors, kept as many of his boys at home as possible. Two of them went away to sea, and seldom returned to the Port. The old man was the head of the house-hold, dividing ·his sway with none. His wife had died when she was yet a young woman, leaving behind her ten children, the eldest of whom, Priscilla, now served in her place, with her husband, Nathan Sawyer, who was perpet-ually "at loggerheads" with the rest of the family. Nathan was a stingy man, much given to quarrelling with his fellow-men, and so ad-dicted to litigation of various kinds that it was a common saying in the two towns that "Nath Sawyer was so terrible fond of lawing that he'd rather go without a meal's vittles than be with-out a lawsuit."

His easy-going brother-in-law, Isaac Grindle, fond of his violin and his comfortable seat by the fireside, could not abide the pragmatic and alert ways of Nathan; and he told his sisters that he could feel his flesh creep whenever he heard Nathan scolding the hired help about the place. The Grindles usually kept at least two hired girls, which was one evidence of forehandedness. And the management of a growing brood of grandchildren—for there were three married daughters in the house — gave employment to many hands.

Isaac steadily refused all advice from his sisters on the subject of marriage. He was what is known in the region as "a likely man," in spite of his easy-going ways. He was as handsome as a young viking, blond, brawny, supple of limb, and gifted with a voice which, when he sang old-fashioned ballads to the music of his violin, moved the hearts of those who heard. Nathan, alone of all the family, could not praise Isaac's melodious strains. And he never could see what good there was "in wastin' so much time over an everlastin' squeakin' fiddle."

But Isaac played and sung serenely on, conscious that he was his father's favorite, and that Nath's growling never came to aught. He did his full share of the work allotted to the various members of the family; and, as the old man proudly said, "kept his end up," whenever there was any laborious task to be gone into by the men on the place. But no rustic gathering was complete without Ike Grindle and his violin. Many a girl renowned for her beauty through all the country-side, where there are not a few beautiful women, had vainly "set her cap" for Isaac. And when it was noised abroad that "Emmy Kench was castin' sheep's-eyes at Ike Grindle," there was indignation and incredulity in many homes where there were pretty and marriageable girls, who never forgot that the Grindles were "forehanded."

Poor Emmy vainly tried her blandishments on Isaac. The handsome young giant smiled on the little coquette, romped with her when the elder people were not looking on, and then turned away to his beloved violin, and straightway forgot her.

If Emmy had any real fondness for Isaac, she concealed it so deep down in her shallow little heart that nobody ever suspected it. And when, after flitting about from household to household, in the widely scattered village of Murchville, Emmy flitted quite away and went off to Camden, the more staid and demure girls of the neighborhood were really glad that she had gone. In those old-fashioned days it was the custom of the country for servants, or "help," to mix much more freely with their social superiors than is now the rule. In the rural villages, especially, hired men and hired women sat at meat with their employers; and this social custom indicated the general freedom with which the two classes mingled on terms of partial equality. So, when Emmy Kench betook herself and her pretty face to Camden, without a word of explanation, the rustic belles of Murchville said they were glad of it. The young fellows, as they came and went about their fishing and farming, said that it was a pity that "gals were so all-fired envious of each other."

Emmy disappeared from the gossip of Murchville and Fairport; old man Grindle died and was buried; Nathan tightened his grip on the household; and then, as if in sheer defence, Isaac married Ruby Ray, a masterful, capable, and managing woman from Bangor.

There was great commotion in Murchville when Isaac brought home his wife; and it is quite possible that many of the younger women fancied that they had been somehow cheated of their rights. But Ruby made friends for herself. Though she was a strong and ruling woman, she had a tender heart and an open hand. She dominated Isaac, and she loved him with all the tenderness of a great nature. New England women are not given to much demonstrativeness. It is not a New England trait to wear one's heart upon the sleeve. But even grim Nathan Sawyer could not help seeing that Ruby adored her husband, in the reticent and self-possessed manner which is peculiar to the people of the region.

Emmy had been gone from Murchville nearly two years, when Captain Parker, of the schooner Two Brothers, arriving from East Thomaston with a load of lime, brought a report that Emmeline was living at Owl's Head, but very near to death's door, and with a child of her own, although she was still unmarried. This news was discussed over many a village tea-table. Captain Parker said, in answer to many inquiries, that the child was "about a year and a half old, and as pooty as a pictur'." This was all he knew about it, except that Emmy, hearing that a Fairport captain was in port, had sent to ask if he would take her back with him. This he could not do; he had no room in his little cabin for a woman passenger with a baby; besides, he was to put in to Northport on his way up the bay, and that would detain him at least a day and a half.

There was much virtuous indignation expressed against Emmy on the part of the villagers; and this broke out afresh, when, one cold November day, as the sloop General Washington hauled up to Tilden's wharf, in Fairport, poor Emmy Kench, looking more dead than alive, was seen huddled in a sunny corner of the deck, with her baby under her shawl. She had come home to die; and the hacking cough, which came now and again from the faded heap that she had made of herself, told of the gradual wasting of the disease which has laid low so many victims to the capricious climate of the coast of Maine.

But where was Emmy's home? The friendless and orphaned girl (for old man Kench had gone the way of all the earth) had no abiding-place anywhere. Then began a dispute as to which of the two towns in which she had lived should be responsible for her support. She was born in Fairport, but she had chiefly dwelt in Murchville. It was from Murchville that she went into another county; so, after much disputation among the selectmen of the two villages, in which the townspeople actively shared, Emmy was "thrown onto" the town of Murchville, the taxpayers of which felt that they had not only been worsted in a wordy duel, but had been imposed upon into the bargain.

And so, to the scene of her former flirtations and triumphs, Emmy had come back to die in the poor-house. Often, when a gay young girl, Emmy had passed by the cheerless poor-farm with a little pang, which she laughed away with her birdlike blitheness. She had half-scoffed at and half-pitied the aged crones who basked on the weather-beaten platform in front of the house in the sunny weather; and she had shivered when she had passed that way in winter, and a thin column of smoke from the chimney bespoke the comfortlessness within; and now she lay dying in the cold north bed-room of the poor-house.

The old clock on the wall ticked solemnly, measuring off in the stillness the last minutes of poor Emmy's life. One old woman, a solitary watcher, nodded over her sewing at the work-house table, on which a candle guttered in its iron candlestick, slowly forming a "winding-sheet" as it died down into darkness. The wail of a child from the bedroom startled the woman, who hastily arose, relighted one of the candles, and hurried into the next room.

"Ma's all cold," whimpered the little one; "and she won't speak to me any more."

The old woman glanced at the clock, and muttered:

"Half an hour yet to dead low-water, and she's clean gone!"

Taking the child in her arms, and stilling its murmurs, as if afraid to disturb the mother, whose ear would never more be thrilled on earth by the cry of her child, the old woman looked steadfastly on the face of the dead. In the awful silence of the night, even to this hardened old creature, who had, in her younger days, "gone out to nuss," the rigid form before her put on a strange pathos. Emmy had rest, at last, from trouble and from sin. She had entered into the mystery of the undiscovered country. The old woman regarded the figure before her with a chilly awe and respect. Death clothes the humblest with sudden dignity.

"The poor cre'tur' died without so much as makin' a sign to tell us who that man was," she whispered to herself. "But I just expect it was somebody in these parts."

So saying she laid the child, now sleeping tranquilly, on the wooden settle in the kitchen, covering him with a ragged quilt. Then she stealthily, and looking around with guilty fears, turned back the bed-covering, and, with shaking hand, took from the dead woman's breast a worn package of letters. These she had often noted when engaged in offices for the sick; and these she rightly guessed contained the jealously guarded secret of poor Emmy. There were only two or three letters, and the watcher had barely time to hide them in her faded gown when the mistress of the poor-house entered. She gave one swift glance at the bed, and said, in a half-whisper:

"So she's gone? And didn't she say anything before she dropped off?"

"Nothin', nothin'," said the other. "She just died as quiet as a lamb. Pore thing! She's gone where there ain't no more sorrer. S'posin' we see if there ain't suthin' hid about her clothes," she added, craftily.

"I hope I know what belongs to my position, Almira Sellers," said the mistress, severely. "Ef there's any s'archin' to be done, it's my business. I'm mistress here."

With a scared look the other drew back and watched the poor-house matron searching carefully through the dead woman's scanty clothing. Nothing was found; and, with a sigh of disappointment, the old woman said:

"Wal, it's died with her. That brat'll never know who his own father was. And I s'pose we may as well lay her out. It's mighty lucky you shif'less old cre'turs got that shroud done in time. And, I declare for't! it ain't two o'clock yet. Wal, the town's rid of one more pauper; and the next thing is to see what'll be done with that everlastin' boy."

And, as if to emphasize this remark, the child on the settle gave forth a prolonged roar.

"Dear suz me!" cried the matron; "do hush that child! He's enough to wake the dead."

But the dead slept on; and the old nurse crooned to the nameless boy a song which told him that he was a "baby buntin'" and "his father had gone a-huntin'."

Emmy's death had solved the difficulty about her maintenance by the town of Murchville. As soon as she was decently buried, proclamation was made through the village that there was a proper man-child at the poor-farm to be adopted by any benevolent or thrifty person who might wish to assume this responsibility, with a view to relieve the town, or to rear up a family drudge. Ruby Grindle, a childless wife, heard of the death at the poor-house with a thrill of satisfaction. She had not wished any harm of the poor girl, to whose latest wants her generous bounty had ministered. But she had coveted the child, a wonderfully handsome boy. Even though she ever had her own will with her easy-going husband, she had not dared to breathe to him anything of the plan which was slowly forming in her mind. But now that the poor waif must be cared for she spoke out.

At first Isaac pooh-poohed the scheme of adoption which Ruby proposed. His brother-in-law, Nathan Sawyer, opposed the suggestion with what seemed unnecessary violence. He would not live in the house which sheltered a beggar's brat, he said. But this opposition only intensified Ruby's determination.

" Nath Sawyer hopes that Ruby'll never have no children,'' said the shrewd gossips, when his angry words were repeated, with additions, through the neighborhood. " And, then, if anything should happen to Ike, Ruby'll only get her thirds ; but if they adopt that 'ere young one, ship-shape and accordin' to law, it's as good as if it was reely their own.''

No mercenary motive influenced the tender heart of Ruby. Her long-pent motherliness went out to the beautiful and friendless boy. Isaac smiled with a certain mannish stolidity, as

Mistress Rogers, in the poor-house kitchen, regarded Ruby fondling the child, and said, "Now don't they make a pooty pictur'?"

It was a pretty picture. Ruby's hair was black, and her solidly moulded face wore that variety of complexion which some call "strawberries-and-cream," but which envious and faded matrons said was "Injun-like." The rosy, flaxen-haired boy, nestling against her cheek, looked like a cherub out of one of Murillo's pictures. The mature beauty of the woman, her face suffused with a newly awakened affection, glorified the tender grace of the child's head, now pillowed on her cheek.

For once Isaac had sided with his brother-in-law. He did not approve of Ruby's plan for adopting the child. He thought it would "only be a pesky bother about the house;" besides, if Nathan disapproved of the scheme he would dislike the boy, and would make trouble for him in the house as he grew up.

"I can defend the child, if you can't," said Ruby, with flashing eyes. "Let Nath Sawyer ever lay a finger on my child, and I'll make him sorry to the end of his life."

So, with the arguments which a strong-hearted and loving wife can use, Ruby had her way. The boy, unconscious of the great change in his destiny which was taking place, was adopted into the comfortable household of the Grindles. The elder sister of the family looked coldly upon the new-comer. Nathan took no pains to conceal his disgust. Isaac, bland and yielding, said, "I hope you'll never be sorry for it, Ruby." But the child throve apace.

WINTER melted into spring, and the short New England summer gave place to another winter. It was a cold and wintry night when Ruby and Isaac sat on the side of the bed in their plainly furnished room in the Grindle mansion. All day long the snow had fallen on the rocky land and into the angry sea. Now the icy edges of the harbor were grinding against the shore, and the black water .was streaked in long patches by the moonlight. The spruces and firs stood grim and dark against the pallid hills over which the snow blew in thin drifts. Across the icy tide of the Bagaduce the town of Fairport gleamed white in the light of the moon. It was a typical New England winter night—a study in black and white. It was a contrast of the deepest darkness and the most ghastly whiteness of light.

In-doors, the farm chamber was cheery and dim. A drift-wood fire burned low on the brick-laid hearth, reddening the old-fashioned andirons and shedding a glow on the whitened wall. The child slept in a crib near the only window, through the green paper shade of which an irregular row of pinholes let in small rays of moonlight, which dazzled from the snow without. On the bedstead, covered with a patchwork quilt of blue and white, sat Isaac, his handsome blond face wet with tears, and his arm half-clasping Ruby's waist.

" Oh, Isaac, Isaac ! " she sighed. " This is dreadful, dreadful ! I wish you had never told me. I'd sooner have died thinking that the baby's father was dead and gone, like poor Emmy ; or that he had wandered off into foreign parts, and never would come back any more ; and now to think that he is really and truly your own child. Oh, Isaac, why did you ever tell me ? "

There were no tears in Ruby's eyes, and she placed her hands, toil-worn and yet shapely, on her husband's shoulders, and pushed him away from her.

" I thought you ought to know, Ruby," the husband answered, as he tried vainly to look into her face, now coldly averted from him. " I thought you ought to know. Nobody in the world had a better right to know than you ; and I'd sooner that nobody in the world should ever know but you. Can't you forgive me,

Ruby? I should have been a better man if I'd 'a' known you then. I never was wild. Even Nath wouldn't say that of me."

He had caught a glance from her eyes. She had not dared to look him in the face—that handsome face which she had so long admired and loved; the handsomest face, as she had often secretly whispered to herself, that there was in the world. She did not trust herself to look into those wonderful blue eyes.

"Say you'll forgive me, Ruby, dear. I've made a clean breast of it. Few other fellows would have done as much. But I could not have you trust me so when I felt that I did not deserve it. So I up and told. And now you won't forgive me. I 'most wish I'd never told on myself."

Ruby turned on him a reproachful glance, and then silently gazed into the smouldering fire of drift-wood.

"What will the neighbors say?"

"Why, you wouldn't tell them, would you? Why, Ruby!" and the man seemed to forget, for the moment, that he was a suitor for pardon.

"No; but I didn't know but that you would think it your duty to tell the minister; and you know the parson is dreadful leaky. No;

I shouldn't want the minister to know, nor the neighbors to know, that I have been coaxed into adopting my own husband's child. Oh, Isaac, Isaac! what a shameful thing!" and the wife's face grew darker in the lessening firelight.

"Ruby! Ruby! How can you have the face to say you were coaxed to adopt the baby? Didn't I stand out agin it? Didn't Nath say you were so dreadful set in your way that you would have that child if all creation was agin you? And now you say you were coaxed to take him in. Oh, Ruby!"

"But you might have told me that he was your baby, Isaac."

"I should have told you, Ruby, if I had known you as well then as I do now." And Isaac dropped his eyes and drew her closer toward him. Ruby resisted, turning her face away. She was obdurate. Her husband, he in whom she had trusted, had deceived her, had concealed his sin from her.

"Oh, I can't! I can't!" she cried. Then, holding her head in her hands, she added, "It has come on me so sudden-like. You must give me time to think."

"All right," said Isaac, still grasping her tightly. "We can send the boy away somewhere, and nobody'll ever know anything about what's happened, or what's the matter."

There was a slight stir in the crib by the window, and the child, turning in his dreams, uttered a low cry and lifted his hands.

With the motherly instinct strong upon her, Ruby hastily disengaged herself from her husband's embrace and ran to the child. His little dream had passed, and he lay smiling in his sleep, his golden hair gleaming on the pillow, and one chubby hand half-open on the coverlet which Ruby had wrought for him, putting into its innumerable stitches and patches innumerable loving prayers. Now she stood over the unconscious boy, clasping her hands and gazing into his face, wherein she traced, for the first time in her life, his father's likeness.

"How like him he is!" she moaned to herself. And her heart went out to the sleeping child. "How like him he is! Why didn't I see it before?"

Isaac sat meekly and in silence on the bedside, watching the waves of emotion chasing each other over the face of his wife. Wringing her hands, sighing, and almost groaning, Ruby stood over the boy, her heart torn with anguish.

"Poor innocent!" she whispered to herself, and the tears gushed from her eyes; which Isaac, perceiving, took courage to himself. She stooped and pressed a passionate kiss upon the lips of the child, dashed the tears from her eyes, ran swiftly to her husband, fell upon his neck, and cried, "For his sake, my darling, I forgive everything."

A gusty blast roared up the chimney, whirling the fire of drift-wood into a cheery blaze. The nine-o'clock bell rang out from the Fairport steeple, its waves of sound rising and falling across the wintry tide. Ruddy shadows crept up the whitewashed wall, and the firelight flickered over the child's crib, by the side of which man and wife stood talking far into the night.

III.

AGAIN the spring had come; and drinking in the balmy fragrance of opening buds of beech and birch, and enjoying the luxury of being out of doors without discomfort, the Grindle family, their day's work done, were grouped on the wooden platform which covered the space betwixt the house and the down-shelving edge of the bluff. The air was humid with warmth and moisture; and in the hollows of the planks, warped by the suns of many summers, stood little pools of water from a recent shower. The sky was white and tender, and gave little reflections in the narrow pools on the platform. The waters of the bay, gray and white in the gathering twilight, their outer rim hidden in the mist, were flecked with flocks of sea-fowl; and clouds of these birds flew noisily from inland over the heads of the group on the platform, and, with much discussion and debate, dropped upon the placid wave.

"Are they coots, Ike?" asked Ruby, following with her eyes the graceful flight of the birds from land to sea.

"Coots, Ruby," replied Isaac. "And it's a sure sign that the heart of winter's broke. The last of the wild geese, I rather guess, went over yesterday. I heard 'em honking in the air all day."

So saying, the strong man lifted the child in his arms, tossing him in the air, telling him to fly with the coots, and light in the water for the night. Nathan looked blackly at the big, joyous man and the laughing boy. "Such nonsense!" he muttered to himself.

The gate in the tall board-fence which separated the yard of the Grindle house from the village road was opened, and Elkanah Woods, town constable, entered, with an air of mingled importance and uneasiness.

"What luck fishing, to-day?" cried Isaac, heartily. "They say the first run of mackerel may be in the bay in a week or two; but I don't think it; it's too early."

"I've got suthin' more important for you than fishin', Ike Grindle," said the constable, with preternatural solemnity. "Suthin' that'll hurt me wuss than it will you, to hand out. But dooty's dooty, and I can't go agin the law."

"Why, what in all natur' have you got?" said Isaac, in a daze.

Taking a long paper from his pocket, Elkanah said, "I've got a warrant for you to appear before Squire Bakeman, to answer a perfectly dreadful charge."

"And what is the charge?" asked Isaac, with a sudden shaking of his heart.

"Bein' as there's ladies present," said Elkanah, with a perceptible blush mantling his weather-beaten cheek, "you'll excuse me from namin' it. But the complaint says that there's proofs in writin', signed by your own name, that you hev acknowledged yourself to be the parent of poor Emmy Kench's child. It galls me awful to say as much, Ike; but thet's what the complaint sez." And Elkanah mopped his honest brow in sheer desperation and discomfort.

"Who brings this complaint?" demanded Isaac.

"Wal, ez near as I can make out, it's your brother-in-law Nath," replied the constable.

Nathan Sawyer had slunk back into the huddled group of the family when this dialogue began; but now, elbowing his way out, he advanced, and said, sullenly, "Yes, Ike, I made the complaint. Somethin' had to be done for the honor of the family, you see. It wouldn't do, you see, to have a motherless brat in the house, and nobody knowin' who he belongs to." And the man shamefacedly turned away.

Isaac, without looking at his wife, whose eyes had all this time been fixed on the restless face of Nathan, said to Elkanah, as if resignedly, "Well, go on; I'll follow you."

The child ran gleefully out of the knot of people in which he had hidden, and cried, "Me, too, papa." At this, Nathan's wife threw her apron over her head and sobbed audibly.

Ruby had not taken her indignant and wrathful gaze from Nathan Sawyer's face. When the child ran to his father and clutched him by the skirt of his coat, Ruby swallowed a great sob, and, with one swift step toward Nathan, shook her finger at him, and cried:

"What do you care for the honor of the Grindle family—you, the leavings and emptyings of the Sawyers? What do you care for the honor of the family—you, who have just gone and blazed abroad the only thing that could have done any dishonor to this family, in which you are no better than an interloper? If anybody's dishonored in this family, I am! If anybody's to be unforgiving, I am that one! But I have known of this thing for months and

months. If anybody has been outraged, I am
that one! And yet, I forgave Ike long ago,
long ago. I forgave Ike when I first knew of
his fault. I bear him no ill thought.'' And
here she choked with an involuntary sob.

Isaac looked on with tears standing in his
great blue eyes. The group on the platform
was hushed as death. Even the child stood
dumb. She went on :

''And you dare to denounce my husband !
—the husband of my love, whose most secret
thought is known to me ; you dare to talk about
the honor of a family ! — the family whose
only disgrace you are trying to publish far
and wide. Get down upon your cowardly
knees, Nath Sawyer, and beg the pardon of
a man whose shoes you are not worthy to
touch ! If there was anything to forgive, I forgave it. Get down, I say, and ask him to forgive you—you, the meanest thing that crawls
—an informer ! ''

She paused, and the hot blood that crim-
soned her face ebbed and flowed in waves that
chased each other from forehead to chin. Nathan hung his head, and muttering something
about the fury of a woman's tongue, sidled into
the house. Turning to the constable, Ruby
demanded of him if it was necessary that her

husband should go with him, then and there, to the office of the justice. Elkanah, evidently relieved by anything that would change the tone of the moral atmosphere, said :

"Land sakes alive, Mis' Grindle ! there ain't no manner of haste. Let Ike come down to-morrer and see the Squire. I'll go bail for Ike, that he ain't a-goin' to run away."

"Run away !" repeated Ruby, scornfully ; "run away ! If anybody runs away, it'll be that sneak—Nath Sawyer. He looks scared enough to run and hide himself anywhere." And Ruby smiled grimly.

"Wal, I reckon he's scared enough to withdraw his complaint," said Elkanah. "And ef I was he, I'd rather do that than hev another such a dressin' daown as you just gi'n him. Land sakes alive, Mis' Grindle ! but you did peel him ! " And Elkanah gazed admiringly at Ruby. Possibly he thought of Mrs. Elkanah Woods, whose sharp tongue was the terror of Murchville, and the one thing of which Elkanah stood in awe.

The sun went down in the clouds and mists of evening, and a chilly breeze was blowing up the bay when the family went indoors. The village constable, as he slowly descended the hill, said to himself :

"She's the all-firedest smartest woman on Penobscot Bay, I swan to man."

Then, as if alarmed lest some wandering sprite might hear his profane soliloquy, Elkanah glanced furtively around and hastened his steps toward home.

Within, Isaac and his wife sat on the bedside, as they had often sat before, and a fire of spruce brush crackled in the low fireplace, for the air of the lagging spring was damp and chill. The boy slept in his crib by the window. The "rote" of the sea came up dreamily from the shores of the bay, and the low wash of waves murmured against the rocky beach below. Heavy footsteps sounded along the entry and up the stairs. The chamber door swung open, and Nathan Sawyer, without ceremony, strode into the room. He was in his shirt-sleeves, and his face bore marks of recent mental conflict.

"I have been havin' it out with Priscilla," he said, doggedly. "Priscilla, she thinks that I ought to withdraw that complaint. Wal, you see it wasn't exactly a complaint, but it was a sort of an information. I thought it my bounden duty, as a member of the family, let alone bein' a member of the church, to have the thing fixed up accordin' to law. Priscilla, she thinks no; you two, I s'pose, think no. Wal,

I don't want any hard feelin's in the family."
And here the man paused awkwardly.

"Go on," said Ruby, calmly; "go on, Nathan Sawyer, and tell us what you propose to do next." She turned to her husband, who looked gloomily into the fire.

"Wal," replied Nathan, "I was thinkin' that if Ike was willin' to give up that note that he holds agin me, I'd drop this business, and say no more about it."

Ruby's eyes snapped an instant, and she said:

"So you'll hush up the honor of the family for the handsome sum of ninety dollars, which you owe Isaac?" And she smiled with bitterness.

"As I said before," replied Nathan, "I don't want any hard feelin's in the family; and I gave Ike that note, you know, for my share of the medder lot, which was Priscilla's, anyhow."

"Pshaw!" cried Ruby, "that's an old family quarrel, and one of your own making. My husband may do as he pleases; but if I were in his place, I would not be party to any such bribery to keep silence."

Nathan turned his eyes upon Isaac, who, with a heavy sigh, rose from the bedside, went to a chest that stood in the corner of the room, unlocked it, and, taking out a leathern pocket-

book, selected from its contents Nathan Sawyer's note. Then, standing before the fire, he
said :

"Nath, I don't know whether you can do
any harm to me and to Ruby and to the boy,"
and here his voice trembled, and he looked
toward the crib. "But seeing that you have
made this offer, man-fashion, I'll take it.
Here's the note; and you'll drop the whole
thing?"

"I'll go down to the Squire's to-morrow
morning, bright and early, and tell him to tear
up the papers." So saying, Nathan slowly tore
up the note into little bits, which he carefully
put into the fire.

"If I had supposed, Ruby, that you knew
anything about this," said Nathan, and here
he glanced furtively at the sleeping child, "I
wouldn't have said a word; but how could I
have ever supposed that you had found it out,
and you and Ike living right on together just as
if nothing had ever happened!"

"So you thought to make trouble between
my husband and myself, did you, Nath Sawyer? Well, I never 'found this out,' as you
call it. Ike told me, like an honest man, as he
is," and the wife's voice faltered a little—"like
an honest man, as he is," she repeated, in a

213

clearer tone, noticing the look of surprise that came into Nathan's face.

Nathan clumsily backed out of the room, latched the door behind him, and went downstairs, saying to himself, as he went : " She beats all natur' ! He told her, and she kept it to herself ! Wal, that gets me everlastingly."

Only a faint gleam of light pervaded the humble chamber, and the fragrant fire of brush-wood died down into ashes, as husband and wife, locked fast hand in hand, stood by the side of the sleeping child.

" I suppose poor Emmy's secret will be all over the village to-morrow," said Isaac, gloomily.

Ruby drew her husband closer to her side ; then touching the child's fair forehead with her fingers, as if she found exquisite enjoyment in contact of her hand and his flesh, she whispered :

" This is my child, Ike ; my boy, my boy ; and I will die rather than any harm shall ever come to him."

And so they stood, whispering with each other, while the last red sparks died out in the ashes of the fire of brush-wood, and the ceaseless murmur of the sea rose and fell in the quiet night.

The Waif of Nautilus Island

THE WAIF OF NAUTILUS ISLAND

"LAND sakes alive! Miah Morey, I'd as live sleep with a log!" And Aunt Thankful sat up in bed, listening to the howling of the storm and the booming undertone of the breakers on Man-o'-War Reef. "I'm sure I hearn a yell," added the irate dame, as she shook her sleepy husband by the shoulder. She peered about the dingy room, which was lighted only by the smouldering coals on the hearth, and listened anxiously for a repetition of the sound which she fancied she had heard in the wild tumult of the March gale that sobbed and shrieked about the island.

With her double-gown over her shoulders, Aunt Thankful opened the door and looked out into the night. Sheets of rain drenched the soggy turf; far out in the watery blackness patches of melting snow gleamed ghastly on the rocky ledges; giant breakers, white with foam, flashed up into sight along the shore, like strange

wild shapes, and then sank suddenly down again.
The angry ocean smote the island with a thunderous hand, and along the reef the hungry
waves showed their white teeth in the blackness
of the night. The air was raw, and drenched
with spume and flying scud ; and through the
thick drift the feeble gleam of the light-house
across the harbor struggled like a yellow stain
in the darkness.

"I haven't seen a wuss night sence we lived
on Nautilus," said the old man, who had joined
the good wife at the door. "The gulls flew low
yesterday, and arter sundown I hearn the loons
hollerin' over to the Cape ; I knowed there wuz
a gale a-brewin'."

"Hold yer clack, can't ye? I can't hear
nothin' for your jaw. Hearken!" And, as
she spoke, a cry of distress came faintly on the
gale from Man-o'-War Reef.

"It's a human critter's cry, as sure as I'm
a' livin' sinner," said Aunt Thankful; and
almost before the words were uttered, she and
her husband, hurrying on their garments, were
struggling against the storm as they ran down
to the reef which made out into Penobscot Bay
from the little island where they had their solitary home.

A huge black hulk loomed out of the sea drift

when they reached the rocky shore, its black sides relieved against the yeasty waves which broke all around.

"It's an East Injiman, out of her reckoning," muttered Miah Morey, when he saw the unwieldy craft, fast wedged upon the outer extremity of the reef.

"God help 'em all," whispered Aunt Thankful; "we can't, in such a sea as this;" and the old couple stood wistfully gazing upon the wreck, as the fierce sea rushed over it and tore it where it lay.

"She's a wrack, sure enough;" and the cooler calculation of the man was turned to consideration of the flotsam and jetsam which the falling tide might bring him.

Longingly and pitifully the old couple looked · across the waste of waters in which no boat could live, and the salt tears trickled down the weather-beaten cheeks of the dame as she heard again and again the despairing halloo of the drowning mariners. Her thoughts were once more with her beloved Reuben, her only son, who had sailed as second mate on a fishing voyage, years ago, and never had been heard of since, though no day ever passed but she cast a weary glance seaward for the white sails of the William and Sally. But they never came.

So she stood there, tearful at last, sheltered behind her husband's stalwart figure, waiting for the end.

"A spar! a spar!" shouted Miah, as a fragment came tumbling through the surf. A line from their fish-flakes, close at hand, was soon around Miah's waist, and Aunt Thankful held the slack, while he plunged in and made for a white object which they saw clinging to the tangle of rigging on the spar. There was a fierce buffet with the breakers, a hurried, sobbing prayer from Aunt Thankful, who saw the strong swimmer reach the plunging bit of timber, and then she screamed through the gale: "'Ware o' the stick, old man; it'll mash ye ef yer not keerful." But Miah had left the spar, and the wiry fingers of his wife tugged nervously at the rope as she hauled him in, hand over hand; and he dragged a heavy burden with him.

Miah, breathless and spent, crawled up the stony beach, pulling the half-clad body of a man. Stooping over her husband and his piteous load, Aunt Thankful beheld a male figure, half dressed as if surprised in sleep, and in its loosening arms, wrapped in a sailor's pea-jacket, an infant.

"The child is alive, as sure as I'm born," said Aunt Thankful, lifting the tiny waif from the figure where it lay. And there, beneath the angry sky, his feet licked by the half-relenting sea which ran far up the shelving shore, the father gasped out the little remnant of his life as his child was gathered to the motherly bosom of her who should henceforth stand instead of those who were no more.

The child wailed while good Aunt Thankful bore her swiftly to her cottage, but soon sank into rosy slumber when, wrapped and warm, she was laid carefully by the side of little Obed, Thankful Morey's orphaned nephew, who slept tranquilly in his trundle bed, happily unmindful of the tragedy which was darkening the coast of Nautilus Island, and casting thereon a mystery which should perplex his life from that hour.

Hurrying back to the shore, Aunt Thankful took the family rum-bottle and warm blankets for the drowned man's relief. But it was vain. No chafing nor restoratives could call back the flutter of the heart.

"He's tripped his anchor, sure," was the figurative speech of Miah, and so they covered him decently, and set themselves to watching for more waifs from the wreck. None came ; and when the gray dawn struggled up in the East, and the sea sank moodily down, the beach was strewn with fragments of the wreck ; and

far out on Man-'o-War Reef only a few bare ribs
of the broken ship, a pitiful sight, thrust their
dark lines up through the rising and falling of
the tide. A low moan came over the remorseful
waves when the rising sun broke redly through
the ragged clouds. The night rack faded away,
and the blue sky looked down on the bay, but
no human sign came up from the secrets of the
sea, save a bit of quarter-board, on which had
been painted the name of the doomed ship.
These were the last three letters of the name—
"USA;" and that was all. And so a great sum
of life and hope melted into the cruel sea and
was heard of no more.

The child was apparently about two years old ;
she knew no name but "Mamie," and took to
her new surroundings as though she had never
known any other.

Curious citizens and eager 'longshoremen
from the little port across the bay came over
and patrolled the edges of the island, looking
for treasures and tragic tokens of the unknown
wreck ; or they rowed around the broken bones
of the mysterious ship when the sea went
down, but found no trace of what she had been,
or under what flag she had sailed. They took
up the form of the dead voyager, and, in
solemn procession, gave it Christian burial on

the bleak hill-top overlooking the harbor, where the people of Fairport exiled their dead. The village squire gathered all available particulars of the wreck into an elaborate account, which, being shorn of its learned length, was duly printed in a Boston newspaper, and, weeks afterward, reached Fairport and Nautilus Island, like a faint echo out of a half-forgotten past. And so all thought of the tragedy melted away from the minds of men.

Only Aunt Thankful and Miah, her husband, kept these things in their hearts ; and even they, as the years rolled on, almost ceased to fear that some one might come out of the great world which lay outside their narrow and secluded life, and, guided by the trinket found on the child's neck, claim and take from them their bright darling, Mamie, child of the sea.

There is no need to tell how Mamie grew into beautiful girlhood, and, never separated from her sturdy playmate Obed, haunted the rocks, spruce thickets, and ledges of the island like an elf. Elfish and uncanny she seemed to the prim townspeople who occasionally came over to Nautilus Island on blueberry parties or fishing excursions. Knowing none but Aunt Thankful, Miah, and Obed, the child was shy of strangers, and, like a timid bird, would fly to

223

the crags and fir-clumps, whence she and Obed looked curiously down on the merry-makers, whose gay clothing contrasted pleasantly with the dull linsey-woolsey and oil-skin garb of the old couple, whom these children thought almost the only people in the world. And strange stories were told in the port of the wild child of the Moreys, and of the heathenish way in which she was brought up to dig clams, rob the gulls' nests, and climb rocks like a young monkey.

But Mamie had a touch of feminine imitativeness withal, and excessively amused the old people by "rigging herself" with wild flowers, sea-weeds, birds' feathers, and flakes of birch bark, in which array she would promenade gravely with Obed up and down the beach, waving her birchen kerchief as a signal to far-off ships which never came, or to careless pleasure-boats that sailed away, unheeding, into the blue depths of Long Island or Cape Rosiere.

Seated on a high black rock near by Man-o'-War Reef, these happy children, unconscious of the mournful tragedies which had given name to island, reef, and rock, in other years, would construct airy fleets out of their own fancies, launch them on the sunny bay, and

sail away into the wonderful world which
lay beneath the sky - rim — far, far beyond
Long Island and Burncoat. To them the distant purple Camden Hills were an enchanted
realm, where the sun set in a palace of gold
and crystal; and away to the southward,
where sky and water met, there was a fairy-
land, whence, once a year, came a richly
freighted ship, which floated up the bay, past
Nautilus Island, and, stately and proud, folded
her snowy wings before the port, and there
dropped anchor. This arrival was a great event
for Fairport; but the ship, which brought to it
a fragrance of the Indies, Cathay, and the
Spice Islands, Madeira wine and Spanish olives,
barbaric, curious things, and a cargo of Cadiz
salt, brought for the two eager-eyed children
on Nautilus Island a wonderful freight from that
enchanted land which they talked of in their
play, and from which some faint sounds had
somehow reached them, and of which they had
some tangible tokens: discarded scraps of
finery from Alicante, and yellow shreds of
lace, handiwork of the nuns of Fayal. How
these faint echoes and little relics reached Nautilus Island we cannot tell. They drifted, as
all such things drift to sea-shore children.

The chief delight of these little ones was the

Bar. This, a long strip of shingly sand, connects the island with Gray's Head, a stony-faced promontory which frowns upon the cove eastward of Nautilus Island. At low tide the Bar is uncovered, and Mamie and Obed loved to run across on the oozy bridge, snatching a fearful joy from the unexplored recesses of the Head, hastening back as the water rose behind them and gushed in eddying rivulets across the narrow tongue of land, licking out the light prints of their fast-flying feet. Barely escaping the rising tide, they would sit breathless on the rocks and watch the waves dashing over their path, running to and fro like sleuth-hounds on the track of the escaping fugitive.

But life was not all play for Mamie and Obed. The old couple, their foster-parents, earned their livelihood by furnishing fish, berries, eggs, and small farm products to the slender market of Fairport. Obed accompanied Miah on his brief voyages into the coves and estuaries about the bay, gathering from the intricate waters which flowed around the many islands of Penobscot Bay their harvest of the sea. The girl, sometimes assisted by her foster-brother, or mother, picked the wild berries of the pastures, dug clams at low tide, and with willing hands assisted Aunt Thankful in the work of the house and little farm. As she grew older she brought to all these tasks a certain airiness which was in odd contrast with her homely toil. She bloomed out in unexpected ways, and puzzled the old dame with her *bizarre* fancies. An indefinable native grace was in all her steps; she loved the bright flowers and soft ferns with which she garlanded her head, and she had an artist's fancy for the delicate shells which formed her necklace. A string of bright India peas which she wore for bracelets were to her beyond all price.

"That air gal will make a smart manter-maker and milliner when she's grown," was Aunt Thankful's frequent remark when she saw how deftly she wrought wonderful snoods and sashes from the odds and ends of woman's attire which she found about the old cottage, or received from occasional visitors from the port. And the distressed old woman wondered if the gypsy-like waywardness and love for bright colors and ornaments which possessed the child were not the tokens of some strain of blood which would, by and by, assert itself, and take her away to the "fine-feathered birds" with which she should mate. No wonder Thankful Morey, knowing nothing but her duty to her "old man," her sordid cares, and her own beloved pipe, grew restive as she watched. "Take off them air rags and tags, you little scarecrow," scolded she, as Mamie, decked with sea-shell necklace, a bit of blue ribbon, a wreath of wild columbines, and an ancient gauze veil and carrying a pumpkin-leaf sunshade, pranced through the house on her way out to a promenade with Obed. The child uttered a little cry of defiance and escaped into the sunshine, followed by a mop-rag which the angry old woman threw after her.

"Dear suz me! old woman, let the gal alone," said Miah, who smoked his pipe on the door-stone. "Ef she enjoys that sort o' thing, let her be, can't ye?"

"Wal, but it duz rile me to see that air gal take on airs. She hasn't half the gumption that Obe has, and the Lord knaows he hasn't got enough to kill. Everybody would 'spose she was born with a silver spoon in her mouth, by the way she carries sail. She's jest a worryin' the life outer me with her antics."

"Wal, now, Thankful, you jest know you wouldn't take a ship-load o' gold for that air gal, and wut's the use o' yer talkin'? Her dressin' comes in her blood, I cal'late; and ef her blood relations was to hev her, I dessay she'd wear furbelows like them high-strung

Boston gals thet wuz over to the port las' summer.''

This sort of speech, which was a long one for the taciturn Miah, never failed to silence the good wife, who dearly loved the girl, with all her wayward and prankish tricks. And when Mamie, discreetly hiding her decorations in the rocks, came in from her breezy walk by the beach, rosy and bright, the undemonstrative but softened dame only said : '' Wal, naow, you are re'ly jest the poottiest little gal on the Bay, I do b'lieve.''

But Obed always took Mamie's part, and when, sobbing and indignant, she sometimes fled from the sharp tongue of her foster-mother, he tried to cheer her in his rough, boyish way, and vowed that when he grew up to be a man he would bring her from foreign parts all the laces and silks that money could buy ; for Obed was to be a sailor and glean the world for Mamie. Smiling through her tears the child would ask : '' And will you really and truly bring me a lace veil and a London doll that opens and shuts its eyes ?''

A solemn promise from Obed gave occasion for a long and delightful confab on things in the future ; and, hand in hand, the children sat on Black Rock, gazing far over the blue, sparkling waters of the bay at the distant sails that floated in the sunny sweep of sky and sea. Happy days! happy dreamers! Alas! that you must ever wake.

When Mamie had grown to be sixteen years old she was a tall, fair girl, with golden hair, shapely as a little queen, with a peachy cheek, and eyes which reminded one of both sea and sky—they were so liquid yet so blue, with an uncertain tint like that of the blue-green wave just off soundings when the sunlight streams through it. The fame of her wonderful beauty had gone out through all the islands, and when, on rare occasions, she rowed across the harbor with Obed and her foster-father, the rustic swains of the port came in groups to admire her from a distance, as she carried her small wares around among the stores of Fairport. Here she caught glimpses of the outer world, and the old-fashioned dry-goods, cheap jewelry, and nameless nothings which decorated the shelves and show-cases of the shops filled her with longings and imaginings unutterable.

Obed guarded her jealously, but the natural manliness of the well-nurtured New England youth protected her from any offence to the half-startled shyness which she bore everywhere. Obed was dark and brown; his hands were hard, and his face had that young-old look which children of toil and poverty wear. But he was brave and loving; and he could row cross-handed, skin a haddock, set a lobster-pot, steer a pinkey, or turn a furrow, with the best man on the Bay. He knew the times and seasons of the mackerel, tomcod, alewives, and smelt; where to find the biggest hake and the sweetest scallops was to him a second nature. He had dived off the village wharf to save a boy from drowning, had picked twelve quarts of huckleberries in a single afternoon, and earned the reputation of being the best salmon-weir builder in all the region round.

But he was nineteen years old, and when, after a short cruise down the Round, he greeted his foster-sister as usual with a tremendous kiss, she blushed and told him, in sweet confusion, that he must not do so again. Grieved and injured, he asked the reason. "We are too old to be kissing each other like babies," and Mamie fled to hide her own embarrassment. That night Obed sat on the rocks alone in the starlight and looked out into the Bay. He watched the waves climb up and down Man-o'-War Reef, and thought of the sweet young life which had been snatched from its hungry jaws; he pondered again the story of her mysterious landing on the island. He looked over at the beacon-light across the harbor, which seemed to blink confidentially upon him as he knew at last that he loved Mamie, and that she might not always be his. He pictured her floating far away somewhere into the wonderful world that seemed to wait for her. The cottage hearth-stone would be unlighted by her gracious presence. Aunt Thankful would forget her temporary asperities, and smoke her pipe in sorrowful silence ; the dingy cabin-walls would be dingier and narrower, and the sunshine would be gone from Nautilus Island. How could he keep it?

But when winter came again, and Mamie went over to the port to attend "the Master's school," it was to supply the deficiencies of education which she felt must not exist when she married Obed in the spring.

Those were happy Saturday afternoons when the stalwart young man, facing his foster-sister crouched in the stern of his wherry, rowed her home to stay until Monday morning. Lovely were those wintry nights when the young couple, pacing the icy beach, looked over the glittering bay, marked the pencil-ray of the light-house pointing afar, hearkened to the nine o'clock bell ringing in the distant village spire, and built anew their castles in the air, dreamed again their golden dreams, and beneath the frosty stars plighted again their undying love.

During the week-days Obed planned fresh surprises for Mamie's Saturday return. He wreathed her bedroom windows with the trailing evergreen from Gray's Head, and strung great festoons of checker-berry and red wild-rose seed-vessels above her little looking-glass. The fragrant juniper with its purple berries perfumed her room, and a wonderful rug of mink and squirrel skins was laid where her dainty feet might most need it.

The humble fare of the family was garnished with its choicest dishes when Mamie came home for Saturday and Sunday ; and on these occasions the picture of the beautiful girl, roughly sketched by a wandering artist who had visited the island, was newly decked with the delicate ferns that Mamie loved best.

This portrait, sketchy though it was, had been a cause of sore trouble once, for the artist, a gay, chattering young fellow from a distant city, while he painted it had talked of the bright world of art, fashion, wealth, and society, and had filled Mamie's head with strange fancies as he drew from her the story of her mysterious childhood. In a moment of unaccustomed ardor she had shown him the locket-portrait which she had worn about her neck when she was found in her dying father's arms. And Obed was angry when he heard the careless artist say that the portrait was that of "a high-bred lady," and must have been painted in foreign parts. But that was all forgotten now, though Obed could never be quite reconciled to the thought that the painter had carried away with him a charming sketch of the Waif of Nautilus Island, painted with the curious locket resting on her bosom.

Spring came, and brought an end to Mamie's schooling. The alders were all a-bloom with their tender catkins, and the trailing arbutus began to gleam in the recesses of the thickets. Here and there, yellow violets sparkled on the wet sod; the bank swallows twittered among the rocks, and the clang of wild-geese resounded far up in the tender mist of the sky. The young folks were across the bar, for the tide was down, and a climb up Gray's Head was not to be resisted on such a day; it was perfect in its cool fragrance and sunny brightness. It was a day to be remembered. It was well remembered.

Dancing and skipping back across the bar, they paused midway to settle an affectionate little dispute.

"So you are sure you would love me just the same if I were worth a meeting-house full of gold?" queried the laughing girl.

Stretching his arms over the little rill of the sea which separated them, streaming across the bar with the rising tide, he answered :

"I should love you if you were a queen on a golden throne, and I were the slave who waited at your foot."

"If you were rich I should not love you, because you would be proud ; " and she vaulted over the swelling current, adjusting the much-vexed question as they went homeward.

At the landing-place they saw a Fairport boat, and, reaching the cottage, they beheld, standing in the middle of the room which served as kitchen, sitting-room, and bedroom for the old couple, a stranger, who held in his hand Mamie's locket. His face was fine and pure ; his air was strangely out of keeping with the humble surroundings, and on him was the aromatic breath of another sphere than that of Nautilus Island. He looked at the stony face of Aunt Thankful, the sad features of the locket-portrait, and on the bewildered, changeful eyes of the girl, and said : "My sister's child ! "

At last the mystery was cleared. The ship Arethusa, bound from Calcutta to Portland,

years ago, carried homeward John Minton,
who had buried his wife in a far-off land, and,
accompanied by a native nurse, had taken his
motherless child to his own country. By what
disastrous chance the ship had been so far diverted from her proper course as to be wrecked
on Man-o'-War Reef, no living man can tell.
But where the good ship Nautilus had been
broken up in 1797, and where a proud Spanish
man-of-war had met its death two years later,
the Arethusa went to pieces on a fatal night in
March, 1846 ; and only this golden-haired girl
remained of all those strong lives which were
whelmed in the breakers of the reef.

The wild, fantastic fancies of the children
had blossomed into reality at last. The tell-
tale artist had showed his picture of the rustic
beauty of Nautilus Island to his friends and patrons in the great city where he wrought. The
likeness to her dead mother, the strange locket
on her breast, the mystery of her birth—all these
had piqued a languid curiosity among the artist's
acquaintances ; but they furnished a chain
which led straight from the gay capital to Miah
Morey's cabin by the shores of the Penobscot.

Why should I dwell on the parting that followed ?

New England people are not given to tears

and scenes, wild bursts of grief and heart-rending farewells. It was settled that Mamie ought to go and see her new-found relatives, while proper steps were taken to secure to her her father's property. Mr. Horton was ready to recognize Obed's right to the hand of his niece, since she claimed that it was a right. But the young man could wait ; Mamie lacked a year and more of being eighteen ; and, meantime, she should take a look at the world before she married and settled down on Nautilus Island ; —and the man of the city looked superciliously about him as he spoke.

So he went over to the port for a day or two while Mamie was prepared for her journey. And there fell a great silence on the household. Mamie and Obed sat on Black Rock, and watched the sea come and go ; she, tearful and trembling, talked of the joyousness of the time when she should come back with her " shipload of gold," to make dear Aunt Thankful and Uncle Miah comfortable to the end of their days. He, jealous and distraught, was half sure she was glad to go. Old Miah mended his nets in silence, and the good wife sternly went about her household duties, feeling, she savagely muttered to herself, " as if there was a funeral in the house."

At last the day came when Obed received the lingering feet of his playmate into his boat; she sobbed once more her farewells on the ample bosom of Aunt Thankful, and kissed the sea-beaten face of old Miah. They shoved off from the familiar landing-place; Mamie turned her eyes, swollen with weeping, to the silent, rigid figures of the aged couple on the shore; Obed grimly choked down a great lump in his throat, and with manly strokes, swept out into the tide which bore them toward the port where the girl's uncle waited to take her to her new home.

When the Bucksport stage, which carried his love away, had climbed Windmill Hill, dazed Obed had rowed back to the island. He plodded in a blind way to the rocks where he and Mamie had sat in childhood, and had built their youthful fancies in the floating clouds. So he sat alone for hours, until he saw, far across the bay, the plume of smoke which marked where the Boston steamboat glided down the coast, bearing from him all that was dear on earth; then he went calmly away, and, with a set face, turned his fish-flakes to the westering sun.

The silent, self-contained household said no word of the day's great event, save, when the nine o'clock bell chimed from the village spire across the tide, Aunt Thankful, as she covered the fire, said: "I cal'late the poor gal is dreffulsea-sick naow."

The days passed wearily. The season advanced rapidly; the leaves rushed out on the trees, and the corn crackled its green blades in the field behind the fish-house; but there was no longer any joy of life on Nautilus Island. Aunt Thankful's "rheumatiz" was worse than usual; and though there was a fine run of salmon that spring, and drift-wood was uncommonly plenty, old Miah felt "diskerridged and clean beat out." Obed worked harder than ever before, but he rowed over to town every night, and waited about the corner until the sound of the post-office horn told him to ask for a letter.

At last it came, that wonderful letter, and the sunset gleams were richer, redder, and more glorious as Obed, drifting with the tide, sat on the thwart where she had often sat with him, and, resting his oars, read her loving words. She was well and happy in her new home. How could she be happy, thought Obed, half in anger; but he was glad to be told that all her bliss was dashed by the thought that she was away from him. She ran on, page after page, describing the Hortons, who lived in a grand house, had servants by the score, with gay equipage and brilliant company. Her aunt was a lovely woman with pink cheeks and waves of real lace. Her only cousin was a handsome young fellow with *such* a splendid mustache ! And would not Obed wear a mustache ? it would become him so. Then there followed many minute inquiries about Aunt Thankful and Uncle Miah. Did the gray duck hatch out well, and was the top-knot hen ready to set yet ? Obed must be sure and not forget her doves ; how did the mackerel season turn out ? And, oh, had he been across the Bar lately ? On the whole, the letter was decided, in family conclave, to be a very satisfactory and altogether grand affair. Obed had a secret pang of jealousy whenever he thought of the handsome city cousin with the matchless mustache ; and he could not exactly see how Mamie could by and by forego the luxurious home which she described, and return to Nautilus Island.

With laborious hands he wrote a reply to her letter, faithfully cataloguing all the domestic incidents which had occurred, and commenting on each as he wrote.

And Mamie ? In her city home she was transfigured by the magic of dress and surroundings. No linsey-woolsey and calico now ; no bizarre sea-weed and cockle-shell decorations. With that wonderful intuition which beautiful women have, she overruled and guided the artistic fancies of her aunt and her millinery women; and the untutored child of the sea-shore arrayed herself in matchless garniture. Soft, bright colors, diaphanous laces and flowing lines were but the unnoticed accessories of the rare loveliness into which she bloomed. Her brown face cleared into rosy alabaster; the sharp lines of her mouth grew soft and full; her glorious hair took on a more golden glow in its bands of pearl and gold. At last her luxurious tastes and her craving for beautiful things were satisfied. Sometimes she stood gravely before the great mirror in her dressing-room, delighting her eyes with the sheen of her silk, the gossamer-like airiness of her rufflings, and she asked if this fair, flower-like creature, so rarely decked, could be the Waif of Nautilus Island? Locking her door securely, she paced statelily up and down her room, learning to sweep with grace her shining drapery, waving her round arms, half hid in lace, and turning her head, as she imagined her beautiful mother in the picture-locket must have walked and moved and turned her lovely head when she was a young girl.

But, in the most ravishing strains of the

grand operas, in the pauses of the gay gossip of
the ball-room, and in the midst of the splendor
of drawing-rooms, her true heart went back to
her own home.   She saw Aunt Thankful spinning in the sun by the door; Uncle Miah
tended his lobster-pots, and thought of his dear
little girl so far away.   And Obed, of course,
he looked across the Bar, and his eye sought
out the ledges in the rocks where they two had
sat and dreamed, or it dwelt lovingly on the
mossy tree trunks among which they had
climbed the Head, seeking for thimble-berries.
With a great longing she longed to go back;
she could not wait another year to hear the beloved voices of the dear ones on the island;
how could she live so long so far away from the
familiar little cabin, the homelike shore, and
the well-remembered wash and murmur of the
sea?

But the city was fair; it was full of life and
beauty for her.   The picture-galleries, the gay
shops, the crowds of well-dressed people, the
delicious opera, gorgeous ball, and occasional
pageant—all these filled her with a great satisfaction.   Under their influences and those of a
refined, luxurious home, she ripened into a
woman of extraordinary beauty and attractive-
ness.   She was the bright particular star of the

fashionable season, and her romantic story, artless ways, and surpassing loveliness filled any
gaps that her unfamiliarity with the gay world's
ways might have made. Men do not readily
adapt themselves to a new sphere of life,
whether it be higher or lower; women have
the art to conceal their unacquaintance with
novel circumstances and soon learn to appear
as though they had never known any other.
Mamie was as one born in the purple.

Obed poured out his strong, loving soul in
long letters, which Mamie read in the rosy,
velvety, curtained privacy of her own apart-
ments with a guilty blush. She was half-afraid
that the stately mirrors and supercilious satin
hangings should discover how dreadfully
crabbed was her lover's handwriting, and how
he misused his capital letters. It was like a
breath from the salt sea to read those dear, loving messages from Nautilus; but, somehow,
her bronze Hebe looked with innocent surprise
from its pedestal when Mamie's rosy fingers
turned over the details of the welfare of the new
litter of pigs, and the promise of the salmon
season. The Louis Quatorze chairs were in-
terested but not pleased with Aunt Thankful's
directions about the yarn stockings and the
catnip tea. The girl was conscious that she

was living two lives—one present and one passing away.

The winter melted, leaving Mamie a little weary; and a summer in the mountains rested her. She saw and loved the snowy, billowy peaks; they reminded her of the familiar white-crested, tumultuous waves that rose over the watery ridge of the sea, or sank into the long level of the placid valleys. The mountains and the great forests were new to this child of the sea, but they oppressed her, and seemed to shut out the sky. She longed for the free expanse of the ocean. So when the time came for her to choose between the capital and Nautilus Island, between her uncle and her foster-parents, she wondered reproachfully that any one could doubt how she would decide; and she astonished the city family by deliberately electing Aunt Thankful and Uncle Miah as her guardians. She would turn her back on the gauds of the gay world, and, with a little sigh for its soft light and color, go back to the rude home of her childhood and to Obed.

There was mourning as well as wonder when this decision was anounced to the city family. And when Obed came out of his life-long seclusion, proud, yet timid, to claim his bride, he was coldly and disdainfully shut into a drawing-room to wait for Mamie. His manliness forbade him to be dismayed by the fairy-like splendors in which he found himself; but his heart sank somewhat as the untutored youth, fresh from the bare, hard life of the Maine sea-coast, contemplated the walls gleaming with treasures of art, the gilded, carved furniture, the heavy drapery, and the multitude of costly objects scattered about in what seemed to him reckless profusion. And when Mamie, blushing and half shy, floated into the room, he was almost appalled. Could this radiant creature, adorned with fragile and costly textures, be his little foster-sister, his affianced bride? The first greeting over, he contemplated her from a distance, hot and cold by turns. He was ready to fall down and worship, yet he was angry that she looked so rare and fine. It was not his Mamie; still it was she whom he adored.

To Mamie, Obed did not look changed; he was browner and a trifle taller; he wore the mustache which she had fancied for him; but it was not becoming, and, somehow, Obed did not "fit into the picture." He did not sit easily on his satin chair; and his garments, awkwardly fitting as they were, were not in keeping with the brocaded drapery behind him. All this ran through the girl's mind, and she vexedly thought how wrong it was to notice them; and yet how much more handsome Obed was in his white duck trousers and blue flannel shirt than in that cheap-looking shiny black coat. Poor Obed! he felt cheap-looking, and longed to be back on Nautilus with his own little girl again.

No word of criticism escaped Mamie's lips. All was well, and a torrent of talk swept away the first natural coolness of restraint which fell on both. There were a thousand things to say and ask, and though, during the two or three days of Obed's stay, she had great difficulty in trying to make him fit into the new life where she was so much at home, she still found her old friend as dear and loving as ever. He was still her Obed!

"I am Cinderella, and the clock strikes twelve," she said, as she laid aside "the fine feathers," and prepared for her return to Nautilus Island. Silk and satin trains were not suitable for her wild runs across the Bar; her laces would not "fit in" with the spruce boughs and wild-brier of Gray's Head. So, amidst great wonder and lamentation in city mansions, she went her way homeward with Obed.

The sunshine, softened and mellowed, came again with Mamie to Nautilus Island. Obed,

proud and happy as a king, conducted his
affianced bride to the old cottage ; Aunt Thankful's hard features relaxed with joyful tears as
she gathered in her arms her restored treasure.
Old Miah sounded his nasal trumpet loudly in
the depths of his bandanna, and turned away,
after a greeting, to split firewood with unnecessary vigor.   The girl brought back with her a
greatly changed demeanor, but she was the
same loving child as of yore.   If she wove into
her quiet browns and grays a stray bit of bright
ribbon or lace, like a *souvenir* of her city life,
it was not out of keeping with the sombre
woods, the dazzling shore, and the blue-green
water that lapped the island.   Her beauty was
heightened by the accidental lights which
gleamed in her quiet dress, and even undemonstrative Thankful Morey was constrained to
say: " Wal, I dew declare you've grown to be
a right proper young gal, and you allers wuz as
pootty as a pink.''

The first excitement of returning over, Mamie
tried to settle contentedly into the old order of
things.   She pranced about the little island
like a child, revisiting all their old haunts, sitting on Black Rock with Obed for a moment,
then darting to the dove-house to call her
pets, visiting the cow-yard to greet the mild-

eyed Brindle, inspecting the fish-flakes, and
listening half attentively to Obed's account
of the net result of last season's catch. But,
most of all, she delighted to chase ácross the
Bar; it was not so easy to climb up Gray's
Head as it once was, but the purple asters were
as bright and the white amaranths as perfect as
ever. The tide came in as it used, lacing the
wet sand with its long streams of frothy spume,
and chasing their steps as they ran to and from
the Head to Nautilus.

Yet, somehow, when she tried to be quite
satisfied with the dear old home, she was morti-
fied and angry with herself that it was not easy
to be so satisfied. Something ailed the place.
It was clear that Aunt Thankful had not been
so scrupulously neat about the house as when
she was a younger woman. She had grown
old and careless in a year and a half. The
rooms were smaller and dingier than when
Mamie went away. The ceilings were low, and
her pure little bedroom smelt of her foster-
mother's pipe. She laughed airily to herself
about all these trifles: she should soon get over
them.

"I cal'late," said Aunt Thankful confidentially to her good man, "that our little gal will
build an L onto the haouse when she and Obe are

married. It'd be nuthin' more'n right, for she's forehanded naow.''

'' Wal, wal, don't less hurry the child; she's noways mean, and 'll dew the right thing when the time comes. I s'pose she'll hev a sight o' money when she squares up with the Hortons?''

'' I don't knaow, but I would like to hev that L built onto the haouse. Mame wants me to git a help; that air Booden gal over to Somes's would be right handy. But no, I don't want none o' the pesky critters raound, breakin' more dishes than they are wuth, and spilin' vittles by the pailful. But I would like to hev that air L onto the haouse.''

Mamie took great pleasure in Obed's manly, resolute ways; he was in refreshing contrast with insipid young gentlemen whom she had known in the city. It was a little trying to her ideas of niceness that he should put his knife to his mouth at table; but then the three-tined steel forks were not just the thing to use as she would like to see him use them. These little non-essentials would be corrected when they were married. Married? She thought of that now with a vague shiver. She was too young yet to take up life for herself. But she was true to Obed; she never, never could love anybody else, for he was noble, loving, and true as steel.

Still, there was no hurry, for she had many
things to do. And one of these things was to
soften down some of the asperities which chafed
her gentle soul about the family. Aunt Thankful must certainly learn to do without that
shocking pipe; and she really did think that
Uncle Miah might shave oftener; his gray stub-
bly beard detracted much from the beauty of
his dear old face, never very handsome.

Aunt Thankful's eyes were not so old but
they were sharp enough to see Mamie's un-
satisfaction. "Wal," she said one day, "ef
ye think them air sheets on yer bed air too
coarse, I s'pose ye knaow where there's finer
ones to be bought. But I hain't got no money
to fool away on such extravagance at my time
o' life."

"O Aunty," pleaded she.

"Wal, wal, my little pink, make 'em dew
for naow; yer'll hev better when yer set up fur
yerself."

These small disputes worried Obed, but
Mamie and he never spoke to each other about
them, and, before they knew it, a thin wall had
risen up between them. It was thin, so thin,
but cold; and they looked at each other through
it. Then he remembered angrily the gentle criti-
cisms which she had passed upon his uncultured

habits. "She's got above us plain folks," he muttered to himself; but he swore roundly at Aunt Thankful one day when she hinted that Mamie was "consider'ble uppish since she had been spiled by them Hortons."

He thought of the wondrous apparition of loveliness that had been revealed to him when he met her in the Horton drawing-room; and he reproached himself that he had been so eager to take her away from a station in life which seemed to have been made for her. After all, was she not the dove in the fish-hawk's nest? But he ground his teeth and kept everything to himself.

Winter came on apace, and Obed coldly consented to a postponement of their marriage until spring. They had long talks now—loving and tender, but sometimes fierce; for the girl had a temper of her own, and Obed was "very aggravating" at times. He was jealous as the grave; she was wilful, prankish, and sometimes teased him until he was frenzied, and she was astonished at her own audacity; but she kept on teasing. And the thin veil of ice betwixt them did not melt.

They were sitting one day on the rocky ledge of Gray's Head, whither they had rowed in Obed's boat. The tide was coming in, and they watched the salt, spongy ice-cakes grinding together as they tumultuously huddled up the Bar. "How lovely this is," she said. "It somehow makes me think of the hurried, crashing, mournful music of an opera I once heard."

"Oh, cuss the opera," said Obed, roughly; for he was in one of his black moods, and she had been unconsciously worrying him. "We've no opera on Nautilus, and I never heard one."

"You shall hear one some day, dear; but I guess we had better go home. Dinner is ready; see, Aunt Thankful has hung the red cloth in the window."

On the way down to the beach, a whim seized her to go across the Bar. "But the tide is coming in, and the ice is running to-day."

"Never mind," said the laughing girl; "I haven't been on the ice-cakes for so long, I want to take a run. You go in the boat and I'll beat you across."

In vain Obed pleaded and in vain commanded. "Will you go in my boat with me? Now or never," he said, meaningly.

"No, and never," she laughed gayly, and fled away, her bright red hood fluttering in the breeze.

Obed took his way sullenly across the cove, making a wide *détour* to reach into clear water.

Mamie went on, her gayety gone—her heart was heavy; she looked yearningly after Obed's retreating form. "Poor boy!" she murmured; "I do not love him as I thought I did. But, before God who pities me, I must keep my word."

She set her teeth firmly as she whispered this to the spectral ice-cakes that came crowding up about her. The way was hard; the tide was flowing in rapidly, and the time she gained in running on the open sand was lost in climbing over the frequent sheets of treacherous ice. The ominous whisper of the sea grew loud and hoarse under the icy shapes that hurried in upon the Bar, hiding her from the shore and from Obed, who was standing up in his boat now and looking for her. Up, up crept the tide, pouring through the blocks of ice and chilling her poor little feet. Her slender hands were torn with the rough crystalline edges of the frozen sea-water over which she toiled; but she struggled on. She was half way across, and could see the fish-flakes on the snowy bank, the old sail-boat hauled up for the winter. How distant they were!

But the tide was rising. She must wade for it, if she got to clear water. Suddenly there was a tremor; the air was hushed and still, save where a little sob crept up from ice-covered Man-o'-War Reef. A jam of ice-floes gave way with a noise like thunder, and great blue and white masses came crowding down across the Bar with the rising tide. Like a drove of hungry wolves, the fantastic shapes sped from shore to shore, sweeping everything before them. There was a little cry as of a human note muffled in the sea, and the icy waves flowed murmurously over the Bar.

Obed's straining eyes saw no graceful figure climb the bank below the cottage; and from Nautilus to Gray's Head the tide coursed in strong, deep currents. Frantic, he pulled his boat through the hindering ice and sprang ashore. No footprints led upward from the island end of the Bar; no form met his distracted vision. Shore and sky, ice, water, and stony-faced precipice looked calmly at him, as he stood, speechless, in his great agony.

The news spread, as such news does, in the air, and from far and wide flocked the rough, compassionate sea-farers of the bay, searching for—it. They never found that for which they sought.

As the sun went down, compassionately tinting the frosty shores with a rosy glow, John Clark, removing his seal-skin cap in deference to a great grief, silently handed Obed a little red hood which he had found on a floating sheet of ice.

And that was all. The Waif of Nautilus Island had returned to the sea whence she came.

A Century Ago

A CENTURY AGO

I.

1777

" THE British have landed at the Back Cove!" shouted Peletiah Wardwell, one fine May morning in 1777, as he burst into the keeping-room of Captain Joe Perkins's house. Dame Perkins dropped her knitting-work, and, looking steadily over her spectacles at the lad, said :

" Peletiah, you have forgotten something."

Peletiah, with a blush mantling his honest and already flushed face, pulled off his sealskin cap and made an awkward bow. Boys were brought up in that way, one hundred years ago.

Then he added, excitedly, but with less boisterousness : " Yes, the British have landed at the Back Cove. Captain Blodgett has called for volunteers."

" And Mr. Perkins has gone off to the Neck," said the dame, rising and going to the window, from which she could look up toward Windmill Hill. No horseman was in sight. There was no sign of her husband's return. Then, with a flash of indignation in her eyes, she turned to the boy and asked:

"Why stand you there? Go! alarm the town!"

The boy was off like a shot.

"What's that? What's that, mother?" cried Oliver, a boy of sixteen, who rushed in from the back garden, where he had been spading up the ground. His mother had taken down Captain Perkins's gun from the wooden mantel where it hung, and was looking at the old flint-lock.

"The red-coats have landed at the Back Cove, my son, and we must defend the town."

"You! mother?" cried the boy, with something like a laugh in his eye, but with his face glowing. "You! mother?"

"The time has come at last, my boy. Father said that there was danger that the British would come over from the Penobscot shore and take the town in the rear. They have landed at the Back Cove. There is no force in the little battery between them and the fort. And Captain Blodgett has only thirty militia-men with him in the fort. Everybody must do his share to save the town. I can run bullets for somebody to use with your father's gun.''

" Give me the gun, mother ! I'll go ! ''— and the lad's eyes sparkled as he spoke.

" Said like a man, my boy ! said like a man ! There are the horns ! '' and just then the sound of fish-horns braying on the village-green showed that the alarm had spread.

The preparations were scant and hurried. Oliver hung his father's powder-horn about his neck, put into his pouch the few bullets he could find, picked the flint of the gun-lock, so that it should not miss fire, and was then ready to fly to the green to report himself for duty.

" I shall run some more bullets and send to you anon," said the mother. " The skillet is on the coals and Dorcas will help me."

The lad lingered an instant in the open door-way, and the sun streaming brightly on him gilded his yellow hair and shed a golden glory over his fair young face. So full of life, so alert and ardent, he seemed for the moment transfig-ured in the eyes of his mother. She went swiftly toward him, kissed him, and without a quaver in her voice said :

" *I* cannot give you to your country, Nolly. God gave you when he gave you a country. You will do your duty."

"That I will, mother," and the boy, throwing his father's gun over his shoulder, ran down the village street to the green.

As he fled, two stalwart fellows hurried by, not forgetting to salute Dame Perkins as they passed. Shading her eyes from the sun, she called after them:

"Seth and Jotham Buker! My little Nolly has gone to the defence. Will you have an eye on his welfare in the fight?"

"Aye! aye!" answered the men cheerily as they ran.

Then Dame Perkins softly closed the door, threw her apron over her head, and sat down on the stair, crying to herself, "My son! my son!"

Dorcas, the little handmaid of the house, brought a bag of bullets, all hot from the moulds, to Oliver as he stood with the other volunteers on the green.

"And I thought, Nolly, that mebbe you'd like your fishin' tackle," and she produced the boy's tom-cod line as she spoke.

The young men standing around laughed at the sight, and Oliver blushed with mortification. It seemed to him that he had grown to manhood since he had fished with that line off the wharf the day before. Curbing his impatience a little, he said:

" Much obliged, Dorcas," and put the reel into his pocket.

" Forward ! march ! " shouted Corporal Hibbard, and the little company stepped out manfully to the tap of the drum, every throb of which seemed to say to the lad : " You will do your duty ! you will do your duty ! " over and over again.

Through the fields they went straight to the crown of the peninsula on which Castine is built. There, on the rounded ridge, overlooking the town on the one side, and the pastures on the other, was a rude earthwork, about ten feet high, surrounded by a ditch, and commanding a view of the harbor in front of the town, as well as of the Back Cove which borders the rocky and sloping pastures behind it. This was " The Fort." Thence they could descry a fleet of boats on the shore of the cove, about a mile and a half away. Half a mile off was a small battery of earth, shaped like a half-moon, behind which a few men might lie concealed and worry an advancing enemy.

" Tell off twenty men for the battery ! " shouted Captain Blodgett.

And Corporal Hibbard went down the line and counted out every other man until he had his twenty men. These stepped out to the front. They were old, middle-aged, and young. Each was afire with zeal; each was more than ready to fight for his country. The oldest was the gray-haired grandsire of Seth and Jotham Buker. The youngest was Oliver Perkins. And as they marched cheerily, yet sedately, down the hill, Oliver's heart beat high with pride, and he seemed to hear a soft voice repeating: " You will do your duty! You will do your duty! "

" Seems to me they might have kep' that little chap at home," muttered old man Buker to his grandson, Seth, discontentedly, though even his aged limbs almost tottered as he spoke. " This is no fit work for children."

" He's grit," said Seth, sententiously, " and I've promised the dame to keep an eye on him."

" No talking in the ranks! " thundered Corporal Hibbard.

The red coats of the British were already gleaming through the firs and cedars as the little squad filed behind the battery and lay down with their guns in position.

" Wait till I give the word," said the corporal, in a hoarse whisper,—" then fire! "

Oliver's breath came fast, and his eyes sparkled with strange light, as the red-coats came steadily on. On they came, first slowly, then, lowering their guns, with gleaming bayonets fixed, they broke into a run, and charged directly upon the battery.

"Fire!" shouted Corporal Hibbard, as he saw the whites of the eyes of the British regulars.

At the word, a rattling crash tore out from the line behind the battery. The enemy's line wavered and broke here and there. Then came a word of command, and the red-coats dashed up the slope, swarmed over the battery, and, in the midst of firing, smoke, and cheers, struggled to gain the position.

It was a brief fight. A few of the patriots managed to escape into the fir thickets to the right and left of the battery, and so fled back to the fort with their ill news.

The British troops re-formed their line and marched on up the hill. How gallantly the patriots defended this last line behind the town, how well they fought, I cannot stay to tell. It was all in vain. When night fell, the red cross of St. George was flying on the flag-staff on the green, and the British colonel was quartered in Dame Perkins's house.

That night Captain Perkins came back and heard the doleful story. " It was a foolish thing to do,'' was all he said. But whether he referred to Oliver's going to the defence, or to Captain Blodgett's attempt to hold the battery, nobody dared to ask. For it was plain that his grief was great.

II.

1877.

"SAY, ma! may n't I go a-fishin' down to the Back Cove, with Joey Gardner?"

Lincoln Parker's mother hung two more of her boy's shirts on the clothes-line before she glanced up at the summer sky, and said:

"Why, my son, it is going to rain, I'm afraid. Besides, there's no good fishing in the Back Cove. Better go down on the wharf."

"Oh, you can catch tom-cods off the rocks, if you only have a long pole. Say, ma, may n't I?"

A few minutes later, Abraham Lincoln Parker, with a luncheon-basket in his hand, was tugging after Jotham Swansdowne Gardner, who was two years older than he and was accounted the most knowing fisherman of all the village lads. The two youngsters cut across the fields, scaled the grassy ruins of the old fort on the hill, and, with a wild cheer of savage joy in freedom, scampered down the pasture which slopes to the Back Cove.

The robins fled away from the newly ploughed ground as the boys approached; and a squirrel that had been scolding at them from the top of Dave Sawyer's fence dropped his tail and scudded away in alarm. Squirrels and robins usually have a wholesome dread of young people, though neither Abe nor Joey was their enemy. These boys had their thoughts on tom-cods, and they scarcely noticed the green and velvety tufts of moss that adorned the pasture-knolls, or saw the pale petals of the May-flowers that sent forth their delicate odors from the very edge of the lingering snow-drifts under the spruce trees.

"Young Dave," as he was called, was ploughing in the little patch which his father had fenced in from the pasture. Summer comes late in Maine, and though this was in warm May, the time for planting had only just begun. The air was full of life. The peewit and the chickadee were complaining in the bushes. The water-spiders and pollywogs were lively in the clear puddles that filled the grassy hollows, and eye-brights and yellow violets were blooming on the swale which is still called "The Battery."

"Hullo, Dave! what's that?" asked Joey, as Dave's ploughshare turned up a brown bowl from the earth. Dave stopped his horses, picked up the bowl, and turning it over in his hands, said : " I swan to man, boys, but that's a human critter's skull ! "

" A skull ! " cried both the boys at once, with eyes agog with awe and wonder.

Abe drew back a little.

"Oh, it wont hurt ye," said Dave. "I reckon this belonged to one of them Revolutionary fellers that fit here, a hundred year ago."

" Fought here, did they ? " cried Joey, eagerly.

" Yes, fit here, they did," said Dave, and he seated himself on the cross-beam of his plough and looked thoughtfully at the brown relic. "I've heerd my gran'ther Dunham tell the story many and many a time. He was into the last war, but *his* father *he* was a Revolutionary pensioner."

" What a little skull for a man ! " remarked Joey. " Should think it must have been a boy."

" Shouldn't wonder ! shouldn't wonder ! And here, you see, is where the British bullet left its mark. Drefful good shot that," and Dave regarded the little round hole with real admiration. " The feller that put that there could knock over that red squirrel just as easy."

" What did they fight for ? " demanded Abe. To him it seemed wicked that people should fight and kill each other, and that this remnant of a cruel war should now be turned up in the midst of the life and beauty of spring.

"Wal! you'll hev to ask your ma about that. She wuz a Perkins, and some of her folks fit into the Revolutionary war. There wuz old Captain Joe Perkins; he wuz your gran'ther Perkins's gran'ther, or great-gran'ther, I don't justly know which. But it was a great fight, anyway."

"A fight for independence," said Jotham, stoutly.

"That's it, Joey. They fit for their country. Many a poor feller bit the dust in that war. They were buried where they fell. But they did their dooty, and it's all the same in a hundred years."

So, tenderly placing the skull on a rock, Dave took up his reins and went on with his ploughing.

"Here's something else!" cried Abe, as the plough moved on. He picked up what appeared to be a ball of dried grass. It fell into powdery dust as he fingered it, and left in the palm of his hand a little bar of lead.

"A tom-cod sinker!" exclaimed Joey. "And that stuff must have been a fish-line. Tom-cod line, d' ye suppose?"

"Don't know," said Dave, who had turned

back to look. " But I know I sha'n't get my stent done afore night if I stop to talk with you boys. Get up, Whitey ! " and Dave drove on.

Abe fastened the strangely found sinker to his line, and the lads went to their fishing in the Back Cove.